KRYSTAL

ZINA

Marie, Zina / Fiction / Krystal

ISBN:

Printed in the United States of America for worldwide distribution.

Edited and formatted by Shaundale Rénā | www.shaundalerena.com.

Krystal is a smart girl with high hopes and big dreams who thought she was doing the right thing by following her parents' wishes and marrying her childhood friend. That is, until finding out his secrets. Will she be able to stay with him, or will she create surprises of her own?

David has good looks and money. He is also living a double life with two different people. Will listening to his family cause him to hit a wall and bring the relationship he wants most to an end, or will he man-up and start making his own decisions?

Meka is a hardcore chick who didn't have a good upbringing. Will giving her all to a man to create the family she never had, but always wanted, take her further down in shambles, or can they resolve their differences?

Carl cannot keep to himself until he one day realizes that stepping out on the one person who is down for you isn't all peaches and cream. Will he be able to fix his relationship, or will old habits die hard and cause him to give up and walk away?

Malcolm has his eye on a diamond. He is willing to jump through hoops to make sure he doesn't lose her. Will he be able to continue fighting for her, or will his own past cause him to slight his future and let her slip through the cracks?

Will these characters be able to make it through the struggles they will ultimately face, or will they let everything fall to pieces?

Chapter 1

Krystal

"Angela, why do I have to do this? I really don't want to."

I tried to plead with my mom for the 30th time, but she was not having it. She wanted me to confess my love for my fiancé in front of family and friends. I would not say I don't love him; we just weren't meant to be together in any way possible. We were the exact opposite. I am a party girl, and he is a good boy. Those relationships never work out.

I eventually came to my senses and looked at Angela, who was probably wondering why I did not want to do this, but my answer did not matter. She and Shirley are best friends; David is Shirley's son. They figured the two of us would be great together since they are like glue to each other. Angela even caters to David like he is her own child. There were a few times when she would take his side over mine.

I went to the bathroom to put on the dress my mom bought me. I looked in the mirror and saw the unhappy reflection of myself. I was miserable in my relationship; apparently, no one else could see that. *Well, I take that back.* My sister could, but that was not going to fly with our parents.

See, our parents are old-school. They picked our husbands, and we are supposed to go with the flow. They *literally* planned out my whole future. They did this for each one of us. My two sisters, Mikiah and Malika, went along with it, but me? I'm not trying to do that. I want to choose my own husband and live the life I want to live.

I pulled my hair into a ponytail, exposing only my arms. Since I only like short dresses, this one bothered me a lot. It was a long, silky, maxi dress that stops at my ankles. I didn't like it but would respect it because Angela picked it out. My mom does not believe in showing skin.

I went to the room and looked through my makeup. I decided on shades of light blue. As I was about to sit down at the vanity mirror, I heard a knock on the door.

"Who is it?"

I heard slurring in David's voice and knew I would be driving home.

"It's me, Baby," David responded.

I unlocked the door and opened it. Unable to read the look on his face, I walked away, rolling my eyes. *I know he came up in here on some bullshit.*

"When did doors start to get locked," David questioned as he put his fingers in quotation marks, "'Around here'?" and started laughing.

I rolled my eyes. "I always lock my door, David. I did not know that's a problem."

"It is because I cannot see what you're doing."

"Why does it matter to you what I am doing?"

David closed the space between us and walked over to me. "Because I care about you, and I want you to have my babies," he stated matter-of-factly.

Surprised, I stepped back and looked at David. I love kids but having some of my own isn't something I was ready to do.

"David," I spoke softly, "calm down. We can wait to have kids."

"No!" he screamed. "I want some now. You must think I am stupid. You are texting other niggas, and you think you about to make a baby with them. You have me all the way fucked up. My first child will be your first child, end of story."

I scrunched my face up but did not say anything else. Hearing someone approach the door, I listened.

"Hey, is everything okay?"

I rolled my eyes because Malika is always trying to be nosy.

"Yes," I responded and went back to doing my makeup.

I could hear my sister's voice through the door. "You know he is not a bad person, Krystal," she said, letting herself in.

David agreed. "See, your sister knows I am a good person. I do not understand why you don't see that Krystal," David screamed.

Malika kept telling him to be quiet, and I kept on doing what I was doing, ignoring the fact David and Malika were in the room. I just wanted this so-called fairytale to be over and done.

"Why do you push everyone away?" Malika inquired. "Why do you go against Mom and Dad's wishes? They just want you to be loved and cared for."

I turned around and looked at Malika. "What are you talking about?" I wanted to know. "I despise their wishes. No one, and I mean no one, will tell me what to do with my life or how to live it."

I sat down at my vanity table, trying my best to deal with David. That is how it was every night, but no one seemed to notice. I turned to finish applying my make-up.

"If you are so worried about him," I told Malika, "why don't you go after him?"

I walked off and went downstairs. Soft music and loud laughter greeted me. I saw a few family members and went to hug them, purposely skipping over her my expected-to-be mother-in-law, Shirley, who did not like me.

"Krystal," someone called. I turned around, knowing it was my cousin, Meka, by her loud voice.

I hugged Mika and admired her outfit. Her husband, Carl, was right behind her, so I hugged him, too. I heard a few whispers, but neither of us cared what was said. Meka then looked me up and down with an 'I know this is not your style' look. I chuckled.

"I know."

Carl let Meka know he was getting a plate and left the two of us alone.

"Are we still on for tonight?" I asked her.

From across the room, "Arrgh," was heard.

Both of us looked up to see David throwing up. *People want me to marry him, and he can't even act right for three hours.* Meka walked as fast as she could and tried to encourage him to get it all out.

"Move back. You do not know what you're doing?" Shirley said, grabbing me by the arm and pushing me out of the way.

"Mrs. Shirley, she is trying to help," Carl protested.

Shirley consoled her son. I knew she also said something to him, but I could care less as I held the arm she had snatched.

"Um, excuse you," Meka added. "You can at least say sorry."

Shirley rolled her eye and looked at Meka. "What if I don't? What are you going to do? Jump me? Huh?"

Meka's face turned red, and I stepped in. "Meka, it is okay. C'mon."

"Snooty bitch," Meka called as she walked off.

Shirley was about to say something else, and Carl stepped in. I decided to grab a plate and go into the dining room.

"Ooh baby, you are rocking that dress." I turned around to see my future husband approaching the table. *Guess he's feeling better considering he was just puking his brains out.*

"So, you mean to tell me you're better *that* fast, David?"

He shook his head up and down like a two-year-old; I saw my mom eye-balling me when he approached. David puckered his lips for a kiss. I stepped back.

"No."

David look confused. "Are you fucking around, Krystal?"

I shook my head in the negative and didn't say anything else. I knew what he wanted, but that was not happening anytime soon.

"Oh, my gosh! Look at you in the dress I brought you. Look at you two. Girl, stand up and show everyone what I bought you," my mother beamed.

I got up and turned around. I started twerking, and Meka began to root while others stared in disbelief.

"Krystal!" Angela called out, causing me to turn around while Meka and I laughed. "Now, I did not raise you like that, and you know better."

"But you did, Mom," Mikiah said out loud.

Angela had a slight attitude. "Krystal, you need to stop disrespecting your mom," her father, Antonio, called out.

I sat down and apologized to both Angela and Antonio, purposely leaving everyone else out due to not caring about what they were saying.

"Everyone, can I have your attention, please?" Angela asked. "We are here to celebrate David and Krystal on their engagement." There was a lot of clapping and cheering. "I am glad she can be with someone who loves and cares for her in a way that Antonio cares for me."

My mom darted eyes at Meka, and I knew she was throwing shade. "I will let Krystal talk, but I would like to thank everyone for coming and feel free to get more food if you want," Angela announced. "Krystal, all eyes on you, baby girl."

I stood up, and so did David. I was nervous as I remained next to him ready to say my speech.

"David, you are the heart beneath my wings. You are everything to me, plus more. When I first met you, I did not want to give you a chance. Now, I am much happier with you. From the sandbox days until now, you always said you were going to be with me. Now, you have gotten your wish.

I pray you will love, protect, and honor me in the same way our parents do each other. David, I pray this marriage will bring us everything we want and then some. I love you, and I cannot imagine being with anyone else."

Once I finished, the room filled with applause. "I think I did a good job," I told myself and sat down again. David hugged me. Everything went back to normal as we sat, ate, and talked amongst ourselves awhile longer.

"I am going to fix us a to-go plate," I whispered to David in his ear.

I got up and went to the kitchen in search of the macaroni salad, my favorite dish. As always, Angela had put her foot in it.

"If you're not happy, then why are you with him?"

Suddenly face-to-face with Carl, Krystal looked around to make sure no one else was within earshot. Carl looked around, too.

"Do you think my parents will be letting me go for anything else? You know how strict they are."

Seeing as the air was clear, Carl continued the conversation, "Well, I would prefer for you to leave than be with someone you don't want to be with," he insisted. "C'mon Krystal, I saw right through you. You might have given a phenomenal speech in the dining room, but I know you 're not happy about doing this."

Carl walked off, leaving me in my thoughts. I finished making the to-go plates and returned to the dining room. David was trying to be social; instead, he was doing the most— irritating me.

"Yeah, there might be a baby coming soon," I heard David tell someone. "I am going to be the best husband and father." Of course, people believed it, but I didn't. I wasn't planning on having his babies.

In all honesty, I did not think I could have kids. Ever since David and I got together, we'd used condoms the first two nights—after that, no condoms, no birth control, or anything else that would have prevented me from getting pregnant. David claimed he went to get checked, and he can have kids. I, however, kept prolonging my appointment.

"You okay, Baby? You have been quiet for a while, and this is not like you."

David looked at me with wondering eyes. I told him yes, praying to God that he would just say okay and back off.

"I know you want some of Daddy's good loving."

I smiled at the amusement he was trying to offer, but I damn sure did not want any of that.

"I'm okay. Besides, we're at my parents' house."

David squeezed my leg; I knew he was serious. Whenever he didn't get his way, he acted like a kid—either squeezing, hitting, or fighting. I knew he would do all of the above if he could.

"Let's go to the bathroom," David said.

I followed, and he was ready to have sex, already pulling his pants down and stroking his dick. I could not keep myself interested at all. My mind drifted often.

I bent over, waiting for my pussy to take a beating. I heard David still stroking himself before he thrust his dick inside me. He was horny at any given time, but when it was time to deliver, he could not keep his dick hard enough to make it through the sex. It was hard, and five minutes later, it was soft again.

Every time that happened, I played it off like I wasn't bothered, but I was. I found herself wanting to have my own needs met but decided to start using toys more often instead. When I tried to talk to David about it, he insisted nothing was wrong.

"My dick is supposed to do that," he always said. "I put it in like it is, and it is your job to keep it hard."

Sooner or later, someone is going to start creating job descriptions for learning how to keep a dick hard. My mind wandered as I opened my legs more.

"Yes, Baby. Go harder, Daddy," I moaned."

I am not going to lie; I was good at faking this type of stuff. Hell, I'd been doing it for two years. I could've been an expert.

"I am about to cum, Krystal."

See, this is what I am talking about. He has always been a two-to-five-minute man. It's embarrassing that we can have sex in bed for not even 10 minutes, and he believes he is the man of the hour when we cannot go that long.

"Yes, Daddy David. Fill me up."

With my commands, he followed. David sat down on the bench by the shower. He grabbed a towel and cleaned himself off, then left. Oh, did I mention he was an arrogant asshole?

I rolled my eyes and grabbed a towel for herself. I cleaned, then checked myself in the mirror to make sure I still looked okay before walking out of the bathroom.

"Oh, are you guys are about to go?" Shirley asked.

I looked around for David. "Yes, we are," I answered his mother.

I could see David grabbing his coat. It was going on 8:30 p.m., and I had somewhere else to be.

"Oh, okay. Drive safe and take beautiful care of my grandbabies." Shirley smiled and went to hug David. She looked at me. "By the way, that was a wonderful speech you gave about my son. I am so proud of how much y'all have progressed."

Shirley touched my hand in a comforting way and walked off as I said bye to everyone else, thanking them for coming.

"Baby, we had a good time tonight," David whispered as he walked up behind me and kissed the back of my neck. I nodded in agreement.

"What's wrong with you?" David asked for the second time during the evening.

"Nothing," I responded.

David blew my answer off, and I was glad he did.

"Are you still going out with your cousins tonight?" David asked in a hurtful voice.

I knew he didn't care for them or me choosing to spend time with them either. It was a shame how quickly he could change the tone. I heard so much hate for my cousins that I just shook my head and nodded yes. It was not a secret that he didn't like them since he suspected they were always in my ear about something. However, that was not the case. We grew up together, so we were just very closed. Mainly me and Meka, we were like sisters. She had actually replaced my sisters because they could be shitless. "Momma don't want you to do this. Momma doesn't want you to do that. Blah. Blah. Blah." They went on and on.

David went into the bathroom that was in our bedroom and shut the door. I knew he was upset, but I didn't get offended when he went out with his cousins for a night and didn't bring his ass back home until the next morning—sometimes afternoon.

I texted Meka and told her to pick me up around 10:45 p.m. I had my bags in place, and Meka already knew what was going to happen. If anybody knew me, they knew I was tired of being stuck at home with that lame-ass finance of mine.

I tried to do stuff with him, but David would not budge. It was like he was ashamed to be outside in public with me; he only wanted to sit in the house and drink his life away. Sometimes, he went over to his brother Aaron's house, but that's about it.

I knocked on the bathroom door and told David that Meka was outside, and she was about to leave. He said nothing, but I heard him moving and the water running, so I knew he heard me. I grabbed my bags and went to enjoy my night.

Chapter 2
David

*D*amn, *I needed this shower, and I will admit I was drunk at Krystal's parents' house.*

I hurried and sobered up. I didn't know what the hell was going on with me. Ever since I got with Krystal, I just work and drink all the time. I know she wants me to do stuff with her, but that's not me.

I heard her say she was leaving and didn't respond. I did not want to come face-to-face with her at all. It was something about her that I could not put my finger on, and it was bothering me. Her vibe was off; it was like she didn't want to be around me, and I couldn't figure out why. I thought maybe she was on her period, but when she let me fuck, that confirmed she wasn't.

I decided to get dressed and go to my brother's house. I knew Aaron would be up, and

I could just crash there for the time being. I walked out the back door and through the alley. They live close, so I spend a lot of time there.

I walked in Aaron's back door and gave him some dap. He did not come to the dinner since he was always working at his trucking company.

"Uncle David," Nico and Melanie ran up to me, yelling.

I hugged my niece and nephew, but of course, Melanie hugged me more. She is an uncle's girl at heart.

"Uncle, Uncle, come here. Let me show you my dollhouse. It is big, and it has everything in there."

Melanie and Roxy turned the corner and laughed. "Girl, you love trying to show off," her mother stated.

I laughed and hugged my sister-in-law, too. "Sometimes, I think she is living better than me," Roxy shared.

I agreed and walked to Melanie's room, where her dollhouse was as big as her wall. I am not going to lie; it was kind of dope.

"Uncle David, why don't Krystal ever come with you when you come to visit us?"

I was still looking at the dollhouse, but I thought about what Melanie asked. *Krystal has been over here once, maybe twice. Every time I come, I am always by myself.*

I got on my knees to look my niece in her eyes. "I don't know Melanie, but I will ask her next time." With that answer, she was happy.

Nico pulled me into his bedroom and showed me his PS4. I played NBA 2K18 with him for a while. That didn't stop Melanie from coming into her brother's room with her baby dolls and their clothes. I made sure they were both asleep before joining their dad.

I found Aaron in his mancave drinking Crown Royal. I proceeded to get myself a cup and sat down on the loveseat across from my brother.

"I talked to Momma, and she told me how the dinner party went," Aaron informed me.

I shook my head because I knew how our mom talked.

"What's going on with you and Krystal?" he inquired.

I shrugged my shoulders. "Man, I do not know. She doesn't want to be around me anymore; she is barely open with me, and honestly, I do not know if I can keep living like this."

"Well, do you think she might be cheating on you?"

"I have thought about that, but I pushed that thought into the back of my head," I admitted to Aaron.

I didn't think Krystal would ever cheat on me when I knew her every move. I had a tracking device on her phone, so whatever she did, I knew where she was.

"Well, that's a thought, but her cousin is another story. Ain't no telling what she is doing, especially around Meka. Bruh, you need to watch her for real. I have heard some things about her."

I agreed with Aaron and answered his phone. "Mom?"

I smiled. If anybody knows me, then they know I am a momma's boy at heart. That doesn't make me soft or anything, but she has always had my back from the sandbox. My dad, Noah, on the other hand, was still trying to call himself "being tuff" on me, but Momma would always protect me.

"I wanted to talk to you about Krystal. She seemed off, and I did not like the way she was treating you. She could have done better."

Mom does not like Krystal because of the stuff I've told her. It was like when we first got together, everyone thought she was going to change into this loving person, and she didn't. I thought Krystal played it well. When she was around her parents and siblings, she was a good girl, but when she was around her cousins, you wouldn't recognize her. She was wild.

"I do not know Mom, but I will talk to her," I sighed.

My mom said okay and asked where Krystal was. She needed some ideas for the wedding and wanted to get her input. I sighed again. I knew I was about to hear mom's mouth.

"She went out with her cousin, Meka."

I could hear her take a breath before she asked, "And you didn't get a location? You know she can be up to nothing good, especially hanging out with that hoodrat. Boy, you need to talk with her. Your fiancé now—wife in six months—should not be out partying while you are sitting at home worrying about her. Did she at least ask you this time?"

I shook my head no like she could see me.

"Oh, wow. Wait until I tell Antonio and Angela about this. I know they are going to flip out, and her twerking at the dinner table was unacceptable. Angela and I had a long talk about her behavior once y'all left."

Mom went on and on about Krystal and how she needed to cater to me. I agreed but could not get her to do that for anything in the world. Krystal was independent and thought I should be too. She was good for the basics, but if I asked more of her, she gave every excuse in the book to not do something.

I reflected on the time when Krystal once told me that if I can do it myself, then I should do it and not wait around for her to get something done. She reminded me that she wasn't my maid or personal assistant. I finished chilling with Aaron and decided to stay in his guest bedroom for the night.

Chapter 3
Krystal

" Bitch, how'd you manage to get out from under David's bitch ass?"

I looked at Meka and laughed as hard as hell. If anybody knew David tried to keep me on lock, it would be my sister-cousin. The shit was funny. I was amazed at what David did just to keep tabs on me. Sometimes it worked; other times, it didn't.

I knew David had a tracking device on my iPhone, so I went to Verizon and acted like something was wrong. I decided to get my own plan and still keep David's. I did not want to give him any reason to investigate. I just used Meka's address instead of my own. Of course, it all came out-of-pocket, but David would never know the difference. He might have thought he was doing something, but I always have my trick of the trades on the side. Meka brought my favorite drink, Cîroc. I knew I was about to be lit.

"I betta not regret this tomorrow morning, Meka," I screamed. *What the hell am I thinking, doing a round two? One party was enough.*

We arrived at Meka's house to get ready. I decided on a black and gold dress that revealed my 44DDs and the tattoos on my legs. I put on gold heels since my dress showed less gold. I took one look in the mirror and admitted I was cute. I was happy for the first time in a long time, and it felt good to be myself again. I decided to wear my hair straight down with a part on the side and added jewelry to complete my look.

Meka was still getting ready, so I grabbed another shot of Cîroc and drank it straight from the bottle. I immediately felt the effects coming on and went to sit down with the bottle next to me. After the third shot, Meka came strolling down the stairs. She looked at me and laughed.

"Krystal, make sure your ass can walk this time. Last time, Briana and I had to carry you out of the club. This time, we gonna leave your ass there."

I laughed. "Y'all gonna come back and get me right?"

This time, Meka laughed, "Yeah, in the morning when your ass is sober."

I took one look at Meka. "Bitch, you look like a lemon."

Briana came in the door. "Bitch, you are about as bright as the damn sun. Where the hell you find that at?" I continued. Meka did not say anything.

"Then you have the nerve to have heels to match the sundress." Meka looked at Briana and laughed.

"Look, bitches, stop talking about me. I guarantee you I will be the brightest motherfucker in the club."

"Yeah, you will be blinging all the hoes," I told her, and we all burst into laughter. "Cmon y'all, let's go."

"Freak Hoe" by Speaker Knockerz came on, and I was damn sure bouncing my ass to every beat of the song.

"That's right; I can twerk and every fucking thing. Shit, I can even fuck on the dick doing a split, but that is a conversation for another day."

Briana came behind me and started grinding. *That got some niggas' attention,* I thought and kept doing my thing. I would see the same people every five-to-six months in the clubs doing any and everything—many of them I went to school with. Now that I was a soon-to-be "loyal wife," it had been at least a year. Some people had bossed up, while others were straight bums.

Even though times had changed, I never pretended not to give even the bum ass niggas attention at one point in my life; it was just never anything serious before my relationship with David. I would not admit I was a hoe, but I received my daily dose of dick.

We made our way through the club to say hey to a few friends, then decided to get something to eat on the other side at the grill. Immediately, a hostess named Ashley seated us where we instantly spotted David's cousin, Nicole, whom I paid no mind. Nicole did not like me, either. She was at the engagement party, but as I said, we did not get along—for the same reason Shirley and I didn't get along: David talked too much.

The noise Nicole and her crew made was obnoxious. We knew they wanted attention, which caught the eyes of some people. They kept looking at our table, but we did not pay them any mind. They started taking pictures and making videos of themselves being goofy, and a dark-skinned man with hazel brown eyes approached our table. He wore a black shirt and black pants with a solid gold chain. I was in awe but figured he had the wrong job. This nigga was fine. Even though he was dark, you could still see his colored tattoos. You could also tell he had a dick print.

"My name is Malcolm," as it said on his name tag. "Can I get you started with something to drink?" he asked.

I ordered Cîroc, light on the ice, and a Pepsi. Meka ordered a margarita, and Briana requested a man like him. Meka and I laughed while Briana held her stare. She was serious. What was really surprising was that Malcolm kept the conversation going. We laughed, and he said he was going to make Briana a special drink. Meka and I looked at her but said nothing.

A few moments later, Meka looked at me. "You must want me to carry you out of this club tonight," she said.

I laughed because I knew she was serious. I was still drinking the bottle Meka had brought earlier, plus another one, and now another. I pretended to faint; Meka died laughing. "Girl, you'd better stop."

Malcolm returned to the table and brought us our drinks. He waited to give Briana hers.

"Taste it and let me know what it tastes like," Meka suggested. We all waited for Briana to take a sip.

"This shit is Pepsi."

Malcolm laughed. "Oh, you thought you were getting a *special* drink?" Malcolm asked in a deep voice.

We laughed again, but Briana was heated. "Aww, you thought you were special, huh?" I teased, pinching Briana's cheeks.

Malcolm grinned, "Can I take your food order, or are y'all okay?"

We gave our food orders, and Malcolm confirmed. "Okay, I will put that in for you."

"Yeah, you are, but you better make sure my food order is right," Briana advised.

"About earlier," Meka started. I rolled my eyes because I knew the shit was fake. "Why did your mom have to pick out that ugly ass dress?"

"Like, hell if I know."

Briana looked at me. "No, she didn't. Let me see it."

Meka pulled out her phone and showed Briana the picture of us standing in the foyer.

"Well, the bows on the dress are cute," Briana said.

Meka snatched her phone away. "Bitch, stop lying. You know damn well that shit is ugly."

I shrugged and took a sip of my drink. "To get the conversation off me, "What's going on with you and Carl? He's been your *boyfriend* for five years. Is there a wedding coming soon?"

I knew the two had been through their ups and downs, sometimes more downs than ups. They were violent as hell, but they somehow made it through each day.

Meka rolled her eyes. "Girl, do you know three different girls called his phone saying they're pregnant?"

Krystal knew that hurt her cousin's soul because Meka was unable to have kids. No matter how many times I told her it would be okay, and she can go other ways about it, she would always get upset.

I did not know Meka's pain. Neither did I know she'd tried everything in the book to conceive; it just didn't work. Meka often found herself looking at baby clothes wondering why she could not have children. I'd told her I would carry her child if she wanted to go that route, but she denied it.

"Are you sure they are his?" I questioned.

Meka shrugged. "I am about ready to throw in the towel with him, Krystal. I know I cannot have kids, but that does not mean to sleep with every female to prove to another female that you can have a baby."

I know, as a female, women do not feel worthy when we are unable to have a child. I felt bad because that's what Meka was going through. *Hell, I was going through it myself. Something told me, David was not the right one to have kids with. If he were, I would have been pregnant by now.*

I got up and went to the other side of the booth to sit by Meka. Briana held Meka's hand. I saw a few tears slip down my cousin's cheek and let her have that moment. She was going through, and she needed it. Even though Carl was good for Meka, he just couldn't stop cheating.

Meka wiped her face. "It's okay, y'all. I will survive."

Meka opened up. She confided in me and Briana about her and Carl sleeping in separate rooms and barely having sex anymore. That was news to me. Meka ate and breathed that man, so she knew this had to be affecting her deeply.

There were times when Carl could not do any wrong in Meka's eyes. If Carl told her those women were lying, that was it; but I knew for a fact at least one of them was pregnant because I was in Aldi's and looked up to see a female shopping with Carl like they were one big family. When he saw me, he tried to explain himself, but I was not trying to hear it. I completed my shopping list that day and left.

Meka was about to go on until I followed her eyes. "Oh, there is that bitch!" she exclaimed.

She heard Meka; everyone did and looked in our direction. We saw that she was pregnant and with three other girls. They were all tall and skinny with some of the same features; something told me they were all related.

I looked over at Meka, and Malcolm was on his way to our table with the food. Meka and Briana sat up and smiled when they were served. Briana thanked him sarcastically for getting her food right. Malcolm laughed, showing his pretty white teeth.

"Damn, he is fine," Briana said. We all agreed.

"So let me tell y'all, Damon had this bitch named Corona to come up to me and confront me about sleeping with him."

We laughed. "Bitch, you mean her name is like the coronavirus that is going around?"

Briana shook her head. "Yes, the bitch is a disease. I am telling y'all."

"Hell no, I would have kicked Damon and Corona to the curve. What kind of shit is that?" I asked.

"So now she is supposed to be pregnant by him, and he sold her this fairy tale ass dream, but listen to this. The nigga doesn't have any money or a job. How the fuck is he going to give this girl a big ass mansion and a brand new car?"

"Wait, ain't he still riding in a 2006, and it's 2020?" asked Meka.

"Yup," Briana replied. "That is the car I gave him to be exact."

"Well, Corona better start seeing the vision and opening her eyes. Better yet, tell her to get a pair of glasses—no alcohol because that will mess up her vision," I offered.

We all laughed. "Corona. People shole know how to come up with names," Meka stated.

Briana looked at her food. "I will have to make sure to give him a big tip if he keeps this up."

After praying over the food, just as I was about to put the mayo on my sandwich, I heard, "Bitch, you gonna act like you don't see me? The fuck? I've been staring at your ass the whole fucking time."

The noise caught me off guard. I was in shock. David's cousin, Nicole, decided to get some balls to confront me like the scary bitch she is. Instead of saying something, I laughed in her face, and Briana followed my lead.

"Bitch, we are waiting for you to step," Meka yelled. She did not play with any bitch, especially when it came to standing her ground. Meka and the other girl started arguing.

"Bitch, what? You need to go back home and learn how to be a good wife," Nicole added, looking around for clarification before they started laughing.

I noticed people recording, so I ignored the cameras and rolled my eyes. I knew David was going to see this before I got home but didn't care. I stood up and walked over to Nicole's booth. I slapped her in her face. Her friend shoved the side of my face, and Meka immediately started hitting the girl.

Nicole grabbed and pulled my hair, attempting to punch me in the face. Briana began hitting Nicole while kicking another girl in the head. Security stepped in, and all of us got pulled apart; we kept swinging. At 5'5" inches tall, my size was not doing anything for a man who was 6'3" and 360 pounds.

Once everything was calm, we asked for to-go boxes for our food. We also thanked the waitress and paid the bill. Once we finished, we got escorted out the door. Briana saw Nicole and her friends in the parking lot and yelled, "Stupid bitches." She argued some more, and I started walking towards them.

"Uh uh, you see that cop right there. C'mon Krystal," Meka urged.

I walked to Meka's car, and Briana followed. "Do y'all know I was ready for round two if they tried it again?"

They were too busy catering to Nicole's hair injury to notice us driving past them. Briana rolled down the windows and threw her drink at Nicole, which landed on her dress. "Bitch," Nicole yelled.

Briana raised the windows. "Bitch, you're lucky my windows are tinted. I know, that's why I do what I do."

Meka and Krystal laughed. "We have to work on you, Briana. You are wild."

We decided to go to Meka's house and stay the night. No one wanted to risk driving home with alcohol in our systems.

Chapter 4
Malcolm

This shit was crazy. Here I was watching the fight from afar. Like how is this possible? *Just to let y'all readers know, I peep everything, and I mean everything.*

I started to go break it up, but I was not in the mood to get punched or slapped today. Have you ever broken up a female fight? When you do, you will not want to break up another one. Not to mention, I just got my dreads retwisted, and I was trying to stay drama-free since a lot of shit has been happening.

Let me introduce myself. I am Malcolm Woodland. Some people describe me as charcoal dark, but I am more dark chocolate. If you stare at me too long, then I can be charcoal black. In addition to my dreads, and I have tattoos all over. Most of them come from the pictures I draw. That's right, my nigga. I am an artist.

"Table 87," I heard. I checked the order then delivered the food to the three beautiful young ladies I had been watching for a while. I didn't think shawty peeped me staring because her older sister, or whoever, was cock- blocking the fuck out of me. She really thought she was going to get a special drink. I gave her ass a straight soda because her ass was thirsty. Honestly, she would have thought I was a creep a long time ago.

"You know you can give all your tips to me," my cousin, Rico, said.

This nigga was a trip, but I chuckled along with him. I came in to help because he was short-staffed, and he could not keep anybody. This nigga done ran through so many waitresses and kitchen staff, the shit was not even funny anymore. It can have a lot to do with Rico's attitude and the way he talks to people. Being that this is my family, I stepped in and helped, but this was not going to be an all-time thing.

I started cleaning tables while continuing to stare at the young lady. She was beautiful. She had a black dress that really showed her titties and thighs. The three of them looked like they favored each other, but I wasn't sure if they were sisters or not.

"Sir, can I please have some water?" I heard.

I finished what I was doing and washed my hands. I got the water and took it back to the customer.

"Here you go, ma'am. Is there anything else I can get for you?" I asked in my naturally deep voice.

The lady nodded her head no and took a look around the restaurant. I was happy it was clearing up and prayed to get out by 3 a.m.

I was always good at figuring out a female. I didn't know if it was that shot of Cîroc she drank, but there was something about her I really liked.

"Go ask her name," Rico suggested.

"Man look, they are having a deep conversation. One of the girls is crying."

I wouldn't dare go over at the time. Besides, Rico knew that was not a possible factor for me. I'll admit, I'm shy. I know I have good looks, but a nigga was not about to be social like that. I would freeze up and straight embarrass myself. Trust me; I did it once.

Honestly, I never had to approach any female because they always came flocking to me. She didn't, but I did not miss the gesture she was throwing my way. That had me wondering if she had a man, or was she trying to play hard to get. I did not see a wedding ring on her finger, so she was probably single.

"Bitch," was what I heard. I saw the girl in the black and gold dress and a girl in a white dress with cowboy boots going at each other's throats. Before anyone could do anything, there was a big fight. I was impressed at the whole thing; no one was backing down, and it was a good one to watch.

I saw security, so I stood back and let them handle everything. When the ladies paid for their meal, I decided to put my number on the back of the receipt, hoping she did not throw it away.

It was almost 4:30 a.m. when I left Rico's restaurant. It could have been sooner, but my cousin's staff was something else. They wanted to half-do the job, and I was not going for it.

I had finished my work already, so I took the time to sit down and rest. Rico tried to make them go back and redo everything, but they weren't listening. When I said it, they did it exactly how they were supposed to. Once Rico was satisfied, then they left.

"Man, you need to start putting your foot down more," I told him.

"Yeah, I know. I don't want them to think I'm mean."

I hated this part of Rico. He could be hardcore when it comes to killing and family, but he was soft as hell working and managing. He needed to learn how to do that and fast.

"Look, Rico, you are not here to be no one's friend. You are here to run a business, and they are your employees," I said. "Now, Rico, your temper matters," I continued, "and you can't be lashing out at random times because things did not go your way. Take a step back and evaluate some things."

"Well, since you know so much, why don't you run the place?" Rico asked.

I laughed. "Man, naw, I am good. That is all you, right there. For real, Rico put your foot down."

I walked off and went to my car. I was tired. "Fuck, man, I need to get home and sleep." I started the car and drove home.

Chapter 5
Krystal

I got home around 3:30 a.m. the following afternoon. Since no one had a chance to eat their food, we decided to go out to lunch and make Meka take us home like she was our taxi driver.

I stood outside and looked at my beautiful two-story house in the suburbs of Chicago with everything I ever dreamed of and more. *How can this house be turned upside down?* I thought.

Many people assume because someone lives in a nice neighborhood and is married, that they are living "the life." They were people on the outside looking in. *Trust me, it is better out than in, sometimes.*

I remembered when David and I purchased this house; back then, it felt like home. Now, I didn't know what it was.

I looked back and told Meka thanks and said bye to Briana. "Call or text me when y'all make it home," I yelled. "Both of you."

Knowing Meka, she would go straight to sleep and tell nobody anything until the next day. I walked to the door and heard the TV. I knew David was up. The smell of cigarette smoke greeted me, and I scrunched my face. David did not smoke, so I was confused as to where this was coming from.

"Hey, David."

David stared at me. "Is this what you wore to the club? Is this the reason you wanted to get dressed at that hoe's house?"

I could not read David's mood, but I knew it was about to take a turn for the worst.

"David, chill out?" I said.

"No, you chill out," he screamed back. "You're going to a club with this little shit on, fighting, cussing, and yelling. Yeah, I got the videos, and you think you are going to make me look bad? Naw, you are a reflection of me shorty."

I laughed. I could not believe David was acting like this. He only got that phrase from a song.

"Look, David, you never want to do anything with me. You want to drink and sit at home. If I suggest something, you are quick to throw it out the window."

David frowned. "How about I throw you out the window?"

I looked at him like he lost his damn mind. "Look, you are not about to touch me, and if you do, you are leaving out of here in a body bag."

I started taking off my heels and earrings. "Now, what you going to do, David? I am sick of you; I am sick of your nothing ass. You want everyone to cater to you, and if you don't get your way, you're calling Mommy."

I was now going through the house, talking loudly.

"Don't bring my momma into this."

"Why not? You call her for everything. She is all in your ear, talking about how I need to be a better wife. Why? The same man has been cheating on her for 29 years."

David slapped me. I touched my face, then picked up a glass and hit him with it. He winced in pain.

"What the fuck?" David yelled.

"I told you, you are not about to be hitting on me. What type of shit is that? Your momma should be sucking your dick instead of me."

"Bitch, you can't even suck dick."

"You're right. I can't, but I am tired of fake-moaning with you."

David's jaw hit the floor.

"By the way, tell your cousin to learn how to keep her hands to herself. Don't forget to be in bed by 3:30 a.m. Oops, I forgot, it is past your bedtime."

With that, I went up the stairs to grab a few items and threw them in my duffle bag. I grabbed my car keys and out the door, I went. I got in my 2016 Audi and looked at my face in the mirror. I could see David on the phone now. I guessed with his mommy, Aaron, or the police. I flicked him off and drove across town to the apartment I kept stashed away for days like this. I knew I could have gone to Meka's or Briana's house but wanted to be by myself for the time being.

When I first got with David, I took care of myself. When we made it official, we leased a house together. David was on me about giving up my apartment, so I told him I did, and he believed it with no questions asked. My grandmother always told me never to put all my eggs into one basket, God rest her soul, and as long as I paid my rent every month, I would be okay.

I pulled in front of a red building and parked my car in the assigned parking spot for tenants. I sat there for a while, contemplating what my next move was going to be. I could not be with David anymore. We weren't even married yet, and he was already throwing a temper tantrum.

I turned off the cell phone David gave me and used the personal one I bought. The only people with the number were Briana and Meka. If anybody else got it, I knew one of them would have to give it out.

I exited the car and threw the old phone on the ground, then picked it up to see if it broke. I grabbed my bags and went to the nearest garbage can and discarded the phone. David might be bold enough to come out here, but he had never been to my apartment. *Out here,* they were good for calling the police. If he decided he wanted to act stupid, he would have to do it at the police station.

I observed my surroundings and grabbed my mace. Walking up the two flights of stairs, I entered my keycode into the lock, checking the mail and grabbing everything I could out of the box. I stuffed my duffel bag as one letter caught my attention, addressed by my cousin Ronny, and proceeded to my apartment.

"Hey."

Immediately, I turned around and stood face-to-face with Malcolm. We gazed at each other for a while then broke the stare.

"Malcolm, right?"

"Yes, Malcolm Woodland."

Malcolm extended his hand, and I introduced myself.

"Krystal... Jackson."

"You married?"

I was taken back by his bluntness and rolled my eyes. "Engaged."

Malcolm noticed my gesture. He said nothing, and I was glad. I did not want to explain this whole engagement to a total stranger.

"So, what are you about to do?" Malcolm asked, now dressed in a pair of dark navy jeans, a navy shirt with a black jacket, and a pair of brown Timberlands.

Here I am still dressed in yesterday's clothes. I shrugged and replied, "I don't know."

"Well, if you don't mind, I can come through."

"Oh, you are so bold."

Malcolm's facial expressions showed that he didn't care, but somewhere inside, he did. "Well, I can come through when he is here. It's just going to be awkward and weird. We can be like three amigos in that bitch."

I laughed. "Why would it be weird if my fiancée is here, and you are just a friend?"

"Friend, huh?"

I could not read Malcolm's expression but knew he was thinking something.

"Do you mind if I still come, or do I have to wait? he asked.

I thought about it. It wouldn't hurt to have a few drinks with a stranger. Besides, there was nothing else going to happen.

I went to my apartment to unlock the door. "Just knock when you are ready."

My apartment was still the same way I left it a month ago. It was clean with just a few dust bunnies as I liked to call them. I'd been over once or twice a month when I wasn't working to clean and make sure everything was still here. I know that when people don't see you in your apartment, they think nobody lives there and are ready to break in.

The only other person who knew about this apartment was Meka, and I knew she would never say anything to anybody. Sometimes, she came to get a break from Carl, and I would do the same with David.

I put my stuff on the couch and checked the place out as always. Then, I undressed and took a hot shower, which always relaxed me. Once I laid down, sleep consumed me.

Boom, boom, boom. I awoke from my sleep and looked at the clock. *8:47 p.m. Why?* I pulled the blanket off and sat on the side of the bed. *Boom, boom, boom.*

I looked out the peephole and saw Malcolm. "Man, you knock like the police."

I unlocked the door, and his cologne immediately greeted me. "Let me find out you went home to freshen up before you came down here," I teased.

Malcolm hunched his shoulders, "You want to see me clean or sweaty?"

I looked confused.

"You want to get turned on or turned off? Your choice."

I laughed and stepped aside to let him in.

"Your place is small."

I did not know whether to take offense to that but played it off. "Well, it is only me here. How much space do I need?"

Malcolm glanced at me, then sat on the couch. "Well, dealing with your 5'3" frame, I would say this is right for you."

Malcolm laughed, and Krystal hit him. "Stop making fun of me because I'm short, Malcolm."

He laughed harder but didn't say anything else about it. "Was you asleep?"

I shook my in the affirmative, up and down, and sat next to Malcolm, "Yes."

As if I hadn't said a word, he asked, "So what are we eating for dinner?"

I raised an eyebrow. "Uh... uh... you were supposed to eat already before you came," I said sarcastically.

Malcolm laughed again and said nothing once more. He got up and went to look through the refrigerator. "You want some BBQ?"

My mouth started watering, and my stomach growled. "Yeah, from where?"

"Put some clothes on; it's a place up north."

I hesitated.

"C'mon Krystal," he said, closing the refrigerator door. It's two friends going out, and then there is a pool hall up the street. I swear, I will have you back by your bedtime."

I stood up to nudge Malcolm, but that didn't do anything because he was a hard body.

"Okay, I'll go."

I was not concerned about being in Malcolm's presence, so I got dressed. Next, I texted Meka and Briana in a group chat to let them know we were going out. Both of them cheered me on. When I texted that I was nervous, they responded in paragraphs.

I made sure I looked okay and brushed my teeth before we went anywhere. The first impression is always the most important, and the first two times, I wasn't looking like anything leaving the club after a fight and coming here in yesterday's clothes. Now, Malcolm saw me in my pajamas. *They say the third time is a charm.*

I rechecked her phone. Meka and Briana had texted back to encourage me to go and not be shy. I was engaged, not married, but for some reason, I thought people had an opinion about everything I did. Even though I was wild, I also considered the odds of meeting Malcolm here and being neighbors.

"You know what, Krystal? You are going to go out and have a good time. You are young, beautiful, and you know your worth. Don't scare this guy away because of what someone else did to you," I told myself in the mirror with a pep talk that seemed to relieve my anxiety. Then I made sure to turn everything off, and we walked outside together.

"Girl, I thought I wasn't ever going to eat."

I laughed.

"By the way, you look beautiful."

I smiled. "Thanks for the compliment, Malcolm."

We walked to a black Chrysler, and Malcolm opened my door. I got in and put on my seatbelt.

"Malcolm, you'd better not kill me with your driving."

"I am about to weave in and out of traffic with you on the passenger side."

"Uhn, uhn. Let me see the aux cord."

Malcolm laughed and gave it to me. He started driving, and I started playing "Fed Baby's" by Moneybagg Yo.

"What you know about this?" Malcolm asked.

To prove a point, I started singing the lyrics word for word. Malcolm joined in.

We arrived at a place called A Pig in the Wall. I unplugged my phone and unbuckled my seat belt as Malcolm walked around the car to open the door for me.

"I heard this place is good," I told him.

"It is. Rib's falling off the bone. I always get the Suicide or Jamaican Me Rub ribs."

"Mmm," Krystal added.

We were seated immediately. A lady named Bethany came to the table to introduce herself. She was a heavyset lady. The thing that turned me off was her wig; it looked like it was holding on for dear life. I looked around and noticed the other workers.

"You mean to tell me, not a soul told her to fix this wig?" I asked.

"What can I get for you ma'am?"

"Water would be nice."

Bethany walked off, and Malcolm laughed. "You know your facial expression tells everything, right?"

I laughed with him. "I bet it does, but that was unattractive on so many levels."

Malcolm laughed some more. Bethany brought our drinks back, and we decided to place our food order. Afterward, Malcolm made small talk.

"Krystal, tell me about you. You are kind of mysterious, but nothing I can put my finger on just yet."

I smiled. Malcolm wasn't the first person to call me mysterious.

"It just takes the right person to find out what the mystery is," I replied.

He looked at me, and for some reason, I nervously stumbled over my words. After taking a deep breath, I admitted, "Okay, so I am a 27-year-old accountant who works at a bank."

"How about you ask me questions, and I will answer them?" Malcolm hinted.

We asked each other questions all night and found out a lot about one another. Once the food came, there wasn't much talking to do. We were both hungry, and the food was delicious. When we finished, Malcolm paid the bill, and we walked down to the pool hall for a round of pool.

"You are good at this, Krystal."

I smiled. "You sound surprised."

I admitted Antonio taught me how to play pool and acknowledged I learned from the best. I was rusty at first, but once I warmed up and got comfortable, I gave Malcolm a run for his money. There were $50 on the table for whoever won.

Malcolm said nothing on the ride home. "I hope you're not sorry about your money," I beamed as I sat across from him on the couch.

I was finally getting to see him in his natural state, and I was ready to find out more. Malcolm had a dark side about him, yet his eyes were glazing as mine wandered across his body. I wanted to ask more questions about his tattoos.

Malcolm chuckled. "Are you just going to stare at me? You are so rude."

My face turned red. "Sorry, I was just admiring you."

He smiled. "Well, I was admiring you, too."

We grinned at each other, which released a little of the tension.

"Why you with a nigga, and you're single in your relationship, Krystal?" Malcolm picked up an earlier conversation.

I laughed but often wondered why I was dealing with David, too. "Honestly, I don't know Malcolm. It is really to make my parents happy."

He raised an eyebrow as she continued. "See, my parents are strict on us. I have two other sisters. Their idea is a man they choose and want us to be with. We just have to deal with whatever. With me, I took their route, but I have always been the party girl." This time, Malcolm wrinkled his nose.

"What, Malcolm?"

"Have you ever thought about going against your parents' wishes?"

I admitted, "Yes, I was thinking about doing that. I just know when I do, I need someone to be loyal and down to ride with me. I will not do it to prove my parents' point. I want someone I know I can trust."

"Okay," Malcolm smiled. "I like that. Finally, a female who wants the same thing I want."

I grinned. "Okay, Mr. Malcolm. It is going on 3:30 a.m."

"Aright, I am about to go home."

We both stood, and Malcolm hugged me. I melted in his arms.

"Shawty, you gotta let go."

I blushed again, face red. Malcolm laughed. "You're cute when you're embarrassed."

I punched him playfully, and Malcolm laughed again. "You want to do breakfast tomorrow?" I offered.

"You mean in six hours? Yeah," Malcolm nodded his head and walked out.

I could still smell Malcolm's scent when he was gone. I checked my phone and decided to tell the girls how the outing went. When they started to reply, I was glad they were still up. That also meant something was going on, and it was their time to talk to each other.

It was 7:32 a.m. when I woke to my phone ringing. *Uggh.* I checked the phone to see Meka calling. Before I could answer the first time, Meka called back a second time.

"Yeah, Meka."

"Krystal, where are you? David has been calling here talking about you went missing in action, and he can't get in touch with you. He is worrying," Meka laughed.

"Meka, you know damn well I am asleep."

"Well, I am calling to tell you what your fiancée told me. Hell, his ass woke me up, too. While we are up," Meka added, "let's go get breakfast."

I groaned. "Meka, I just want to sleep."

"Krystal, c'mon. We can go shopping and stuff. Why sleep your life away?"

I chuckled. "Okay, only because you forced me to."

I took off my engagement ring and placed it in my armrest. Then I decided to send David a "we need to talk text." He instantly called after that, but I let it go to voicemail and sent another text with a time and a place. Of course, David sent back a paragraph. By then, it was whatever.

I texted Meka, letting her know I was at the restaurant we agreed on for breakfast. When I walked in, she was already sitting at a table with drinks.

"Fat ass," I stated and sat down.

Meka laughed. I already knew she did not play about her food. We immediately started to play catch up when we finished our meal.

"Meka, come with me to the house to get my clothes and some more stuff."

She followed me, and we noticed a blue sedan sitting in the driveway. Meka got out and started to investigate.

"Meka, chill. There has to be an explanation."

I knew my cousin would get wild, and I was trying to keep her sane because I wanted to know what was going on, too. I had looked inside the car and saw female products and a car seat. I walked towards the door and pressed my ear to it. The TV was going, and someone was yelling, "Dad."

"Oh, hell, naw."

I put my key in the lock and turned it. Then I walked in to see David hugged up with one of the girls from the restaurant with Nicole. He hopped up off the couch and quickly ran to me.

"Krystal, baby, I am sorry," he pleaded. "She is just a friend."

"Friend?" the girl yelled out.

David turned around and gave her a look. She smacked her lips, and I slapped David.

"You cheating on me, David? You want everyone to think you are this good person... how you do all this stuff for me, etc... But you are a low-life bum," I yelled.

David put his hands up in surrender. "Daddy," one of the little boys called and brought David something he drew.

"You have kids, David?"

David put his hands down in shame. I started hitting him, and the girl pushed me off of him. I landed on the floor.

"Bertha!" David yelled.

"Bertha?"

Meka charged at her, immediately punching her in the mouth, as I continued to go after David. I hit and called him names while the kids were screaming, but I didn't care. They weren't my kids.

I heard something slam onto the ground with a hard thud. "You stupid bitch," Bertha yelled out.

Meka laughed as she spat on Bertha. David ran to her rescue and realized she was lying on a pile of glass. Then, he started fighting Meka, and I joined in to help her.

I felt my body getting pulled, and I was thrown into a wall. It didn't take a rocket scientist to realize someone had called the police; I was scared by a longshot. I just didn't want whatever they were going to charge me with on my record.

"Stupid bitch," David shouted out.

"Stop acting like one then, bitch," I retorted and walked past David, spitting on him.

David continued to say all types of stuff while the police did nothing. Since it was Thursday, the court hearing was the next day. They wanted to charge me with breaking-and-entering, criminal damage to property, and disturbing the peace. I beat all three charged and was free to go, so was Meka. I just had a restitution fee to pay come Monday.

Carl met us outside the police station. "Aww, look at the criminals now."

We both laughed as Meka swayed her way to Carl, kissing and hugging him. He hugged me, too.

"Damn, the last two I thought I would see in jail."

Carl dropped Meka and me off at our cars, which were still at David's since he wasn't getting released until Monday. Within an hour, we had gotten all my stuff out of the house. By the time I, Carl, and Meka finished, my car was full.

"You'd better not buy anything else, Krystal. Like, for real. You have a lot of shit. Hell, I thought I had a lot. What's crazy is I don't even see you in the shit."

We all laughed, and I hugged Meka and Carl. I thanked them before they went home.

"What the heck are you doing here with him?" Angela asked me.

I looked at my mom. My dad was right behind her.

"Mom, why does it matter, and how did you find out I was seeing someone else and where I live?"

Angela got closer to me. "Baby girl, I know everything. You flaunting around with this man is not going to cut it for us."

I grimaced.

"Krystal, why can't you just listen to Mom and Dad for once? Whoever the guy is, he's bad news. David is the one for you," my sister chimed in.

I got up. "Uh, nope. David has kids and a girl, and he has been lying to me about who he is. Nope, I am not doing it."

"Krystal, Krystal... sometimes you have to consider people's flaws like they were your own."

"Mom, do you *really* think I am about to go back to that man after what he did to me? Really, if you did..."

"If I did what, Krystal?" Angela asked. "David loves you."

I laughed, "Yeah, sure he does. You seem like you like him more than me. Why not make him your son?"

"Don't be silly, Krystal," Antonio said. "We love you just as much as the other children."

"Well, Krystal, if you weren't so heavy in the belly, and stopped having sex with everyone in the club, maybe you could've started a family," my other sister jumped in.

"Look, I am going to date who I want. There is not a chance in hell that I'm getting back with David."

Antonio laughed, "Well, you know that means you are no longer part of this family."

I shrugged my shoulders. "You're saying it like that was going to change my mind. This man has shown me more loyalty than my own family." I pointed at Malcolm, who was standing by the door, and Angela took a step back.

"Well, I hope you choose wisely. We don't allow people back in once they are out," she warned.

"Well, she got me," said Malcolm.

"Sir, this is family business. I am going to ask you to leave."

"Naw, Antonio, he can stay. You can leave."

Antonio and Malika walked out together.

"Krystal, I am very disappointed in you. We haven't done anything but given you a good life, and you are ruining it by being with this guy."

I shrugged again. At this point, I did not care anymore. "Mom," I spoke.

"No, to you, it's Angela."

"Oh, okay," I acknowledged. "David and I are not together. There is no need for you to keep bringing his name up."

"Krystal, you are not part of this family, and David is. As you said, David can be our new son, so he took your place. I hope you have fun with everything."

Angela walked out the door, and I blew out a breath I didn't know I was holding in.

"Thank you, Malcolm."

Malcolm sat next to me and pulled me closer. "Krystal, I am down for you if you are down with me. I know we're still in the talking stage, but I am here to build you up and help you out. You down to ride?"

I shook Malcolm's hand and hugged him. "Thank you again."

Malcolm shrugged it off, and I got up to look outside. That's when I saw Angela and Antonio talking with my neighbor, Kenya, and giving her money.

"I live right there, so this is a good spot for me to tell you everything," I overheard.

I became angrier by the second. Kenya looked up and covered her mouth. Angela and Antonio looked up, too, as I closed the curtains.

"What's up?" Malcolm asked.

I hesitated before telling him everything. Malcolm got up to see a black sedan pulling out the parking lot.

"That your people's car?"

"Yeah," I answered.

"They've been over here a lot. I thought they moved in or something."

Chapter 6
Meka

*T*he shit that comes around me is beyond me.

I prayed every night, even on my knees. For some strange reason, karma finds its way back to me, and I do not like it.

After David left Krystal's house, I called Krystal to see what was going on. I knew she made it into the house because I dropped her off, but David told me they'd argued. Krystal paid just as many bills as he did in that house, so I could count on one hand what the argument could be over. To be honest, I didn't know why Krystal had stayed with the coward. I knew at the engagement dinner at her parents' house the shit was fake; it just wasn't for me to speak on.

Krystal answered on the third ring in a low voice like something was bothering her. To be honest, I was glad she was okay because David's ass acted like she went M.I.A with no return address. Well, she did, but that wasn't the point. They argued, and he wanted sympathy. If he knew any better, he knew I was the wrong person to come to for encouragement. To add to that, I don't like him.

"Hey girl, where you at?"

I had a confused look on my face because they were at a restaurant, and I was hungry.

"Red Lobster," Krystal informed me.

"Oh, can you please bring me back some butter biscuits? I will love you forever."

Krystal laughed. "Always trying to bribe me with some food," she said.

Honestly, I am not missing any meals over here. I'm chubby, and I'm not afraid to show it. I think it looks sexy at times.

"What's wrong?" I heard a guy ask in the background.

"Hey, I am back," Krystal said.

I scrunched my face up in confusion. *How did this happen? Shit. David was looking for her, and she was on a date with another man.*

"Krystal," I called her name. "Who is that?"

She turned the phone to the guy we saw at the restaurant, and this man looks even better without his work clothes on. He had me almost ready to drop my underwear. Let me stop, and y'all snitches better not tell Carl nothing.

When Krystal returned to the phone, I told her I would hit her back later and do not forget about my biscuits. Once I made sure she was okay, I looked up, and Carl was standing by the wall looking at me. I could not read his facial expression, so I couldn't tell you what type of mood he was in. I just gave him my undivided attention like I always did.

"You know the baby is mine?"

It did not take a brain surgeon for me to find out what Carl was talking about. I got up and went to the bathroom. Carl tried to stop me from leaving, but I moved his hands and continued walking.

Here I am looking in the mirror at a pretty individual who is possibly damaged goods. I'm light-skinned and 5'7". I've got some weight on me, but I wear it well. I can also hide it well if I want to. I have a successful career, too. What more could anyone, more specifically Carl, ask for? *Oh, a fucking baby.*

"I'm not able to have kids," I told myself in the mirror, but that made me look crazy, so I stopped and sat on the tub. When Carl found out I could not have kids, that is when the cheating started.

Niggas will tell you, "Oh, it is no problem. We will get through this?" Well, this will be his third baby momma, and I am looking dumb because I am sticking with him through it all. It hurts because all of his kids are stair-steppers. The oldest one is three. I have never told Carl the reason that I cannot have kids, but he never asked me about it either.

I wiped my tears and cleaned my face with a towel. I walked out of the bathroom and was face-to-face with Carl. He did not budge, and I was kind of scared. When Carl gets upsets, he is a whole new person I barely recognized. I don't know why he is upset when he got himself into his predicament.

When I got up from the couch and went to the bathroom, I knew that bothered him. He would always say we need to talk it out instead of us walking off and staying mad at each other. To be honest, I thought Carl wanted to see her down at her lowest.

"So, you just going to walk away from me while I was talking to you?" Carl asked.

I shifted my body to the right side and looked at this nigga like he was crazy.

"Carl, what could I possibly sit there and listen to you say? You said you had another son or daughter. What else could you want from me? To keep letting you make kids with other women? Carl, this is your third baby momma in three years, and we have been together for five. So, let's do the math. Five years minus three years equals two, but you have probably been fucking with bitches for that long, too."

"Well, if you could have kids, then I would not be out here doing what I do," he responded.

That struck a nerve because I dealt with it daily, but I was not letting him give me another excuse for why he was cheating. I walked past Carl and went into the room we shared. I pulled out a duffle bag and started to pack some items.

Carl looked at me, and I continued to pack while he was standing there. Once I finished, I walked past him and took one last look at the man I loved. I took the ring off and put it back in his hand.

"I am sure there is someone out there who can meet your needs."

With that, I walked out the door without looking back and checked myself into the Hilton Hotel. I decided to stay there a couple of nights before I headed to Detroit. I'm an interior designer who loves my job and makes good money doing it. It's now to the point where clients come back to me for additional projects, and I offer them discounts.

I went to the room and immediately started crying. I could not believe I would be going through this.

"Uggh," I cursed myself. "Why me, God? I want a family. I pray every day and every night. I am healthy; I had a man. What more do you want from me, God?"

I got up and laid on the bed, glad I worked the next day to keep my mind off Carl. My phone started to ring *again*, and I let it go straight to voicemail.

Chapter 7
Krystal

"Can I get butter biscuits to go?" I asked our waitress?

Malcolm laughed because he knew why I was ordering them. "How long you and your girl been cool?"

"That's my cousin, and since she came into my family."

Malcolm raised an eyebrow.

"Meka was 14 when she came to live with my aunt," I explained. "She's adopted."

Truth be told, when I first met Meka, I could not stand her. Once I found out more about her, we became road dawgs and have been together ever since.

Malcolm nodded his head. "Well, I have two brothers and one sister: different dads, same mom. I never knew my dad, but I know he's locked up. Every time I asked questions about him, my mom cut me off. I didn't know him, but I did know I wanted better, so I own a private business."

"What business is that?"

Malcolm looked me in the eyes and told me, "I am a hitman."

I gasped but tried to remain unfazed. "Wait, are you here to kill me?"

Malcolm laughed hard, which got the attention of other people. "No, I am not here to do that. I am here to be on a date with a beautiful girl named Krystal."

I blushed. "Aww, well, I am enjoying my date with a handsome guy named Malcolm."

The waitress brought the biscuits to our table in a to-go bag along with the new check. Of course, she couldn't let the biscuits be free.

I hugged Malcolm when we stood. "I had fun with you, even if we just went out to eat and walked around the park. It was something fun." *There had been plenty of times when I wanted David to show me off, but that was an epic fail.*

"These hugs are going to stop, girl."

"Okay," I let go and started kissing him.

"Okay, okay. I see you," he responded. "Your cousin wants her biscuits for real."

I nudged him. "Uggh, I hate when Meka doesn't answer. Yes, she wants the biscuits."

I called Carl, and the call went straight to voicemail. "Shoot, man. They love doing this."

"Ooh, they can be getting it in," Malcolm cited.

"I see you took your funny pill today," I countered. Then my phone rang.

"Meka, where are you?"

I was taken back by her voice. "I am at the Hilton. I will get the biscuits tomorrow."

"Meka, what the hell happened?"

She was sniffling. "Krystal, it's okay. I will come to your place in the morning if that is cool with you."

I agreed. Meka hung up, and I looked at Malcolm. "Well. I guess we can go home then."

"Krystal, I'm sorry," Kenya yelled from across the street. Malcolm instinctively hopped on guard as she ran towards us.

"They lied to me, Krystal," Kenya tried to plead. I put my hand up, but she did not get the message. She kept talking.

"Kenya," I screamed. "I do not care. Don't tell me anything about what you and my parents had going on. I do not care."

Kenya's face frowned. "Really, Krystal? You've always been boogie, like for real. Your parents tried to protect you, and you have not done anything but turn your back on them."

Kenya walked off, and Malcolm stopped her. "Hey, cmon."

Krystal stood off to the side.

"Why do you always believe everything someone says? You think her parents gave a damn about her and what she wanted? Naw, not at all shawty. As soon as she tried to do her own thing, they backed out on her and walked away. I mean, we would appreciate it if you don't come around and tell us about her parents."

Kenya took a step back and looked at me. "Krystal? Really? You're going to let him talk to me like this?"

I shrugged my shoulders. Once Kenya did what she did, I did not care. It was apparent she got paid to do it. I walked off, and Malcolm followed.

"Thank you, Malcolm. I just don't want to get you involved in my drama."

"Krystal," Malcolm whispered in a low tone, "you are not getting me involved in anything. I just hope you are as loyal to me as I am to you. I just ask for the same in return."

I looked Malcolm in the eyes, "Baby, you have my word."

I went inside my apartment, glad to sit down. My phone rang, and the CallerID showed "Meka" across the screen.

"Krystal," Meka said, "this dirty motherfucker had another baby on me. Like how is this shit possible?"

I heard Meka scrambling around, my own heart, broken.

"Then this motherfucker had the nerve to say that if I could have kids, then he wouldn't cheat."

"Nah'un, Meka. Let's go beat his ass. Like for real, that shit is foul. Like, why would he say something like that?"

Meka took a deep breath. "It is okay, Krystal. I gave him his ring back. I am tired. I gave my all to this man. I told him secrets, and he still did me wrong," Meka explained. "Krystal, when he went back and forth to jail, who was there?"

I sighed. Meka had been down with Carl since the first date they had. I liked Carl but wanted to beat him up.

"I'm sorry, Meka."

"Girl, it's cool," Meka said. "I'm about to travel. I just received three more interior design gigs."

I smiled. Meka's good at what she does. "Ooh, cousin, make that money."

"You know it, Krystal."

"Oh, by the way, Malcolm took your biscuits."

Meka gasped. "Fat motherfucker. He knew those were mine."

I laughed. "I guarantee you are mean-mugging right now."

"You better love that nigga, Krystal. If y'all ever break up, I am beating his ass years from now. I do not care if it is 20 or 30 years from now."

I talked to Meka until it was time for her to go. "Talk to you later, and be safe."

Chapter 8
David

Yeah, I got the call from my cousin. It was all set up. I told Nicole to follow her and see where they were going and what they were doing. Once everything popped off, I was expecting her to come home, but she did not show her face till the next fucking morning. The shit infuriated me.

To my surprise, what she had on did not make it any better. Krystal was annoyed and drunk. She did not care about anything else at the moment. I planned to go to Meka's house and talk to her. My mom was right about her needing to be a better wife and stay home. I thought a lot about this, and a lot was about to change.

I pulled up to Meka's house, but I did not see Carl's or Krystal's cars outside. I understand what y'all are thinking. *Why is he trying to be with Krystal after what he did?*

To be honest, I was in love with Krystal. I love Bertha, too, though. She had my kids. I just wasn't expecting Krystal to find out the way she did. I knew when everything went haywire that I had to try harder to get her back.

I got out of my 2016 Jeep wrangler and grabbed the flowers I bought Krystal. I proceeded to the door and knocked about three times before Carl opened the door. The look he gave me let me know he was ready to throw down if said one thing wrong.

"I'm here to see my future wife."

Carl looked at me. "She's not here."

I glanced at him in return, "You're lying."

Amused, Carl stepped aside. "See for yourself."

I walked in and looked around. I checked the entire house. "Fuck, man, where did she go?"

Carl stared at me and said nothing.

"Carl, you sure they're not hiding?"

"Really, David? Hiding? What the fuck you think? We are grown, ass people. Who in the fuck has time to play Hide and Seek?"

Fuck, man. Carl did have a point. "A'ight, Carl. I'm leaving."

Carl watched me leave the house in silence and closed the door behind him.

"Well damn, he could at least wait till I got to the car," I said to myself.

I had more to worry about at the moment than Carl; I needed to find Krystal. After pulling into a local gas station to fill up, I decided to call Angela and her sisters. I even considered Antonio and her other cousins. *I even checked her damn Facebook.*

I had inboxed Krystal, but after 20 minutes, I got mad and called her on Facebook Messenger. After three attempts, I Face-Timed and repeatedly called her for 30 minutes, but the calls went straight to voicemail. I finally gave in.

"Malcolm," I heard Angela say on the phone, "I just saw my daughter, and she was not wearing a ring."

I rubbed my forehead and frowned. Krystal always wore her ring, no matter what she was doing.

"Listen, David. She had another guy there," Angela continued, "and she took his word over her own parents."

What pissed me off was that she was with another nigga, like for real.

"I'm guessing you know where Krystal is," I stated calmly.

"Yes, Kenya and Briana have been keeping me in the loop about Krystal and Meka's whereabouts." *Briana. That's who I need to talk to.*

Angela started telling me how Krystal was acting a fool. I was stuck on how she did not have a ring on. I'm telling you, what angered me most was that Krystal had another guy around her. She was showing her ass; I did not approve of anything she was doing.

"Angela, where is she located?"

Angela gave me an address, and I entered it in my maps app. *Man, I told her to get rid of that apartment.*

Angela scuffed, "Well, you know she doesn't listen... Hang on."

I waited. "David, this is Briana. Let me get the story from her, and I will give you a callback."

Chapter 9
Krystal

Today was a busy day at work. Everything I didn't get done on Friday got piled on my desk. Monday's load got added to it. *I have to get this done today, or my boss will be on my ass tomorrow.*

As an accountant, I handle all the numbers, and heavy shit, people didn't want to do at the bank. That was the reason I went to school; some people did that job for years. By being the new person, they assigned me whatever they wanted and then tried to take the credit for getting it done.

I reflected. It had been three years ago when I started at Corpers Teller Corporation. I was out of college with a master's in Business Administration. There were two older ladies when I joined the team. One was about to retire, and the other still had some years to go. While training with Mrs. Becky, the other lady did her job. When she left, all the work got put on me. *That's what happens when you're new.*

I busted my ass to make sure I met my deadlines, and that old two-faced, raggedy-mouthed ass bitch, told the boss how she did this and that. My chunky black ass jumped right in and busted her bubble. After that, we were feuding. Still, to this day, we are feuding, and that was three years ago.

I got up from my desk to take a break before I got into the craziness of the day. An unknown number crossed the LCD screen, which I decided not to answer. When it came across again, I hesitated.

Moments later, I heard a deep, baritone voice. *The day just got worse.*

"Krystal, bro, you tripping. Where are you?" David screamed into the phone.

There was a female saying something, and David immediately started yelling, "Briana, shut up and let me handle this."

My bottom lip fell when my heart dropped. *No...* There had to be another explanation for this. *That could not be Briana, my cousin. Naw, naw... She wouldn't do anything like that to me,* I thought.

David was as sorry as they come. Like seriously, who still texted and stalked a person once they realized what they did was wrong? Day after day, the texts became threatening, and I found it funny.

"Bring your ass home, or you're going to lose your spot in the bed."

I laughed for at least 20 minutes. I already lost my spot in bed. To be honest, my "spot" was never there, to begin with. Who the fuck was he going to give it to, the girl from the restaurant?

On top of that, I had a feeling David was also was fucking his assistant. Anytime I would go to his job to have lunch or to do anything with *my fiancée,* she would give me a sorry ass excuse. I was not leaving, and I let her know every time she let something stupid out of her mouth.

I walked outside and took a deep breath; it's something I had to do when I got stressed. I didn't smoke but would try a blunt right now.

A black Range Rover pulled up, and I immediately knew who it was. *David.* I watched him get out of the vehicle and walk towards me.

"Oh, you got a haircut, David. It looks nice on you."

David ignored my sarcasm. "You just gonna leave and not tell nobody where you were going?"

I looked around. "What do you mean, leave? You're acting like a little boy, David. You know why I left. You tried to argue and put your hands on me. What did you expect?"

"Man, I been looking for your ass all weekend, and I have to come to your workplace to find you."

"Yup," I responded. "You should have been looking for your girl. Not running behind me trying to watch my every move."

David nodded his head and walked off, then turned back around. "Bring your ass home tonight, and leave that nigga alone. You heard me?"

"Well, if I come back, my new nigga will have to come also."

This time, David looked around. "Krystal, I am your husband."

"No, you mean *fiancée,*" I interrupted, "and we are not going any farther than that. We are now associates."

David walked back towards me. "Is there a problem?" I blurted out.

David shook his head.

"Here, you are telling me to leave somebody alone when you barely do your job at home," I laughed.

David was mad as but hell, but I was telling the truth.

"Krystal, I am going to be your husband. You are supposed to take care of me. You are supposed to make sure your womanly duties get done. I should not ever have to cook, pick up a broom, or clean anything. My mom did it for years, and my parents are married, so I expect the same from you."

I stared at David. "You must have smoked too much weed, or you got into some good crack. Do you really think I will be doing all of that while you are sitting on your ass? Nigga, I have to fake-moan every time we have sex. How is me being any less of a woman more important than you being any less of a man? Your 'manly duties,'" Krystal finally took a breath, "are supposed to satisfy your woman, and you failed at that."

David said nothing, but I knew I'd gotten under his skin. I was tired of him trying to control me. It was becoming sickening.

"Don't come running back to me when that nigga breaks your heart," David shouted and walked off without saying another word.

A group of people had witnessed the entire scene; I knew they heard everything. The only thing they would do is gossip.

"Find some business!" I yelled before taking a deep breath and going back to work. *Lord knows I do not want this information to get out.*

Chapter 10
David

*P*issed *was an understatement.* I had been looking for *that woman...* my *fiancée* ... all weekend and just so happened, I had to pull up on her ass at work.

Krystal didn't even seem a bit phased at all, to me. I would not be lying if I said I wasn't worried because I wasn't. I checked all my bank transactions and my credit and debit cards, and she had not accessed any one of them. That let me know she had some secret shit going on, and I was going to get to the bottom of it.

I entered through the back door and walked up five flights of stairs to my office. I did not want to see or be bothered with anyone at that moment. It would require questions, and questions needed answers. As an attorney, I wasn't ready for that.

"Straighten up my cases for the day," I told my assistant when I saw her.

I sat in my chair and looked at my degree. *A master's in Business Administration,* I smiled to myself. *I've come along way.*

I thought about my time with Krystal. We became close while studying at Clark Atlanta University and worked on a group project. Out of six people in the group, we all had separate assignments, yet when everybody paired up, Krystal and I were the last team.

Krystal was calm and quiet. I told my mom about her—like she didn't know already. My mom just listened to me. Her sisters, on the other hand, were *way* cool. A year and a half into our relationship, I decided to make her my fiancée.

I was brought back to reality by a knock on the door.

"Come in."

Lela, my assistant, came into my office, smelling like strawberries. She shut the door and took off her jacket, then leaned over to put something on the desk. I took in her DD breasts.

Lela was smart; she knew when to do it and how. After loosening my belt, she unbuttoned my pants and pulled my man out, then quickly went to work. I tried not to be too loud as she was moaning, but she could tell it was long overdue.

"Do you need anything else, Mr. David?" Lela asked once she finished.

I shook my head, no, and watched her put my dick back in my pants.

"I will be back for more," she whispered in my ear and walked away, leaving me in my thoughts.

******

It was going on 9:30 p.m., and I was about to catch a case. I told Krystal to be here tonight.

Still, she was nowhere to be found. Plus, she blocked me from her phone but kept me on social media for whatever reason. I called her on Facebook Messenger another three times before she walked through the door with some nigga behind her. She did not have any clothes nor a duffle bag with her.

"Where's your duffle bag? In the trunk? Go, get it. I know you have clothes to wash."

"Nope, I am good."

Krystal blew me off with her hand, but I had to remain calm. "Who the fuck is this, Krystal?"

"David, I told you that I was not coming here unless my new Biggs was coming with me. Like it or not, either you accept it, or we are done."

I surrendered. I wanted to talk to Krystal alone, but all of that was falling on deaf ears.

"Let's talk about the last time, Krystal."

She raised an eyebrow.

"What made you fight my cousin? I asked.

"She was talking shit. She came to our table on some other shit, and Meka and I were not having it. I looked at her because I could have sworn that girl had another head."

"You know we don't fight family."

"That is your family. She is *your* people. She does not respect me, but you are too fucking blind to see the shit."

I was appalled, but she did have a point. "Okay, I will do better."

"You always say you will do better, but when and where are you going to do it? Your mom fucking hates me, and I think your dad feels sorry for me, so he's just nice to me. Your people are phony, kicking it in my face. I cannot deal."

"Speaking of my mother, you need to learn how to be a better wife before this wedding."

She gave me a look that I could not read, but I could tell her blood was boiling.

"A better wife? Nigga, I ain't even made it to your wife yet. Hell, as I told you earlier, we are associates. Once I took that right off, it was over."

The dude with Krystal had his eyes on me. He looked like if I said the wrong thing, he would jump, so I let her finish.

"You ought to be out your fucking mind. Nigga, I work like you do. I cook and clean and make sure your laundry is fucking done, and you want me to be a better wife. And stop letting your mother tell you what I need to do. How about she say that to me and not send messages."

With that Krystal got up and walked off. I let her have her space, as I sat there deep in my feelings.

Chapter 11
Krystal

I was not upset at all. I knew this was all coming, but I did not expect it to go this far. Malcolm and I were laying down in the fully furnished basement tonight, so we did not have to deal with David. He kept peeking his head downstairs but never said anything. David thought he had one over on me; this was my house just as much as it was his.

"Daddy," I heard.

I laughed because I knew David was trying to be petty.

"Damn, the nigga got a woman who looks bad."

Malcolm showed me Bertha's Facebook profile picture, and it wasn't flattering. The kids came downstairs and stopped in their tracks. David followed them and sat on the edge of the couch.

"Krystal, what the hell is going on?" he demanded.

I laughed, damn near choking on my drink.

"Hey, you little fat fucker, why you eat my biscuits?"

I handed Malcolm the phone.

"See, what happened was..." Malcolm started to plead.

Meka laughed, "Naw, naw... I want my one. You knew I wanted those biscuits, and I was hungry."

Malcolm chuckled and handed the phone back to me.

"Daddy, can you do this for me?"

Meka said she grimaced through the phone the minute she heard reference to David. "Keep calm," she told herself.

"I'll call you back, Meka," I told her.

We all sat in the basement and watched TV for a while. When everyone went upstairs, and I heard the door close, I nudged Malcolm.

"What, Krystal?"

"Malcolm, I want some dick."

He laughed. "Krystal, go to sleep. You're just trying to get payback."

"Malcolm, what is your purpose in this?"

He laid on his back. I climbed on top of him, then chilled out. I then started kissing him on his neck and cheeks.

"Shit," Malcolm groaned. "Krystal, shit."

I released Malcolm's manhood from his basketball shorts. Then I looked at him and started to go to town with my mouth moving up and down.

"Damn, Krystal."

Malcolm tried to push my head further down, but I didn't need any help. I took it upon myself to go deeper. Then, I got up and undressed.

"C'mon, follow me," I instructed.

I went to the bathroom in the basement. I turned the water on, being careful not to make it hot. I then grabbed my soap and got in the shower. Malcolm followed behind me.

I lathered and washed Malcolm's body entirely, seducing him in the process. He followed my lead and put soap on my body, letting his hands take care of the rest.

Malcolm played with his already rock hard dick. I sat on it, taking in inches I didn't even know I could handle.

"Shit, Malcolm."

Malcolm kissed me. I could feel my pussy walls tightening while he continued to go back and forth inside me.

"Damn, Krystal," Malcolm whispered, his voice low and deep.

I tried to get off because I felt myself cumming, but Malcolm thrashed my insides with harder thrusts.

"Ooh, Malcolm... Baby, uggh."

"Say my name, Baby," Malcolm commanded.

Malcolm sewed his seed inside me. We both sat on the bathroom bench and tried to catch our breath. Ten minutes later, we got up to wash ourselves off again and laid down to go straight to sleep.

Chapter 12
Malcolm

" Bruh, what the fuck? Man, move over," I yelled to my nephew. We were currently playing 2k18, and I was getting my ass whooped. I was getting hotter by the second because we had at least $100 on the game. I threw my hands in surrender and gave my little cousin the money.

I know what y'all want to hear. Yes, Krystal and I are still fucking around. *Lowkey, I'm feeling her.* I'm breaking down those walls, and there is no telling what's going to happen after last night in the shower. I'm surprised her so-called fiancée let all that shit go down.

For a minute, I thought Krystal was going to tell me to leave and stuff. But, naw, she held me down and even confronted the nigga. I just don't understand that shit and how the nigga said nothing. Then he was trying to bring his family over, and I paid they ass no attention.

"I have to go check on Grandma. Don't cheat next time, either."

I pulled up to my mom's house. I silently prayed she was there. I'd heard she had been acting a fool lately—having men over, taking trips, and not getting home until 3:30 in the morning like she was my damn age or something. I got heated with that one. People had hit me with, "Well, you know y'all are grown, so she only has to worry about herself." *Blah Blah Blah.* I didn't want to hear that.

I got out of my Chrysler and went to knock on the door. I used the spare key when nobody answered. The sight in front of me was unbelievable.

"Mom! What the hell are you doing?"

My mom popped up, and so did my Uncle Ray's head along with my dad's. A nigga was in disbelief. Something told me to leave, but I wanted answers. *This nigga is my uncle—a man I look up to for advice when I need to vent.*

"Do you know how many times I came to this nigga for advice about girls?" I asked myself. Uncle Ray had never turned me down for help and always talked to me, but to see him and my momma together was an understatement.

"Malcolm, I can explain," Mom gasped, mortified and shocked that I was there.

I looked at her waiting for it. I needed her to explain, big time.

"Malcolm, Avery is not your real father," she confessed. "Your father is incarnated. His name is James Woodland. Sorry, you have to find out like this."

I looked at my mother in disbelief. I had never been the type to disrespect any woman, especially the woman who brought me into this world, so with thoughts flooding my mind, I didn't know what to say and left the same way he came in.

I got back in my car and looked at the picture of my birth father and me; my mom had hidden the photo when I was younger. At first, it was in an album. When I got older, I started asking questions about it. Then one day, I was looking for it, and it just up and disappeared.

I waited until my mom was gone and started to look for it again. She had a treasure chest that she put all of her important documents in. I checked it, and there was the missing picture. I took it and hid it from her; something told me he was my dad.

I looked just like the man in the picture. What was funny was how my mom always tried to say Avery was my dad. That explained him taking my siblings to the ice cream shack and leaving me home, or while everyone else always got new clothes, I got hand me downs. I was so angry that I hit the steering will. I was never the type to cry, but my mama could have told me the truth.

I looked up to her, standing on the porch in a robe. She didn't even have the nerve to put clothes on. I started my car and drove off. I could have gotten out to get more answers, but being this upset, nothing was going to go well. I had to sleep on this one.

Chapter 13
Carl

" C'mon, girl. You are always doing this."

That was the third argument Riya and I had this week. I would try to get my son, and she would always come up with an excuse, then get on Facebook and talk about me like I didn't just try to take care of Jaheim, Jr.

One day I screenshot all the messages and posted them on her page. I bet she got the attention she wanted then. She ended up deleting the posts she'd made once people started inboxing and bashing her. That did not stop anyone from reposting the screenshots at all, though.

"Daddy," Jaheim, Jr. yelled.

Carl picked up his namesake and kissed his son on the forehead. "Carl Jaheim Woodland, Jr."

The boy looked at his mom and smiled. She knew what that meant.

"C'mon Jaheim. You are going to your cousin's party."

I could not get Riya to act right for shit. Every time I came to get him, it was something. Jaheim had to do this; Jaheim had to do that. *Blah Blah Blah.* I was getting fed up with the excuses.

"Why I can't take him? You are only going to take him to your cousin's to leave him over there for a night while you do only God knows what."

Riya looked at me. "Don't worry about what I will do with my child. Worry about why your bitch can't have a baby," she smirked.

Riya knew that was the reason I had cheated with her. That shit struck a nerve. No matter what Meka and I went through, I did not allow anyone to disrespect her.

At that moment, I realized I talk too much and should have kept some things to myself. Now it was coming back to bite me in the ass. I put Jaheim, Jr. down and told him to get his coat. Then I got in Riya's face.

"Do you want your ass whooped?"

Riya stepped back.

"I didn't think so. You already know if Meka finds out about any of this," I told her, pointing to her stomach, "she will whoop your ass, and I am breaking nothing up. Baby or no baby, before you speak on a situation, make sure you know what you are talking about," I told her. "For future reference, the bitch got a name, and it is Meka. Better yet, *you* call her TaMeka. We are using full government names around this bitch," I said and stepped back.

I watched Jaheim put on his coat and grabbed him. I was heated but also glad I could leave with my son. I grabbed his stuff and put it in the car while Jaheim buckled his seatbelt.

It amazed me how much he had advanced within the last three years. It felt like yesterday when I was just holding him, making a promise always to protect him.

I was now in the driver's seat. I knew Riya was feeling some type of way but didn't care. Honestly, I also knew I should have kept my dick to myself. Meka had been down for everything with me. I couldn't even blame her for walking out; I was just hurt and felt betrayed by it. For the last two weeks, I've been thinking about her and wondering if maybe she deserves someone better.

I decided to FaceTime Meka, and to my surprise, she answered. Meka was just as beautiful as the day I first met her. Her skin was glowing, and her long curly hair was now straight. We stared at each other until I told her to hold on.

"Here, Jaheim."

My little boy looked at the screen and immediately started smiling. If it was one thing, Meka loved Jaheim, Jr.—anybody around her could tell you that. Jaheim instantly started talking to Meka as if she was his mom. He told her everything, not leaving one detail out. After 10 minutes of driving, I pulled into a gas station and told him to say good-bye to Meka, then grabbed the phone.

"We need to talk," I told Meka.

"Why? Why me?"

I asked Meka to hold on as we got out of the car and went into the gas station.

"Dad, can I get Sour Patch Kids, please, and juice?"

"Yeah, sure, whatever you want," I answered, catching the eyes of a few women, but there was nothing more amazing than Meka on FaceTime.

"Get me a brisk, Carl," Meka stated.

I returned my attention to the screen. "Your ass is in Detroit. How the hell are you going to get it?"

"C'mon, Carl. You are going to bring it to me. It's only a 2-hour drive," Meka claimed.

"It is a 12-hour drive, plus two."

Meka laughed. "So, I will get it tomorrow then."

I smoothed my eyebrows and smiled. "For real, Meka?"

"For real, Carl."

We stood in line to check out. I handed Jaheim, Jr. his tablet and headphones. When they were on and connected, I looked at the Meka.

"I should drink your brisk since I know you are not coming home."

Meka laughed again. "Look, my stuff is packed, but it will only be for a few days."

"Baby, I am sorry," Carl apologized.

Meka got up and went to the bathroom. She turned the screen, and it showed three pregnancy lines. I smiled.

"That's yours, Meka? Like, legit yours?" I asked her.

She shook her head, "Yes."

My smile got even bigger.

"Please, Carl, don't tell no one yet. I just want to make sure everything will happen for good."

"Okay, Meka. I can do that. I know you don't want to get your hopes up for nothing."

For years doctors told us she could not have kids because of her cervix, and if she did get pregnant, a baby would not make it past four months in the womb. We'd even looked into a surrogate mother and adoption, but I knew Meka wanted the real thing. She wanted to experience the emotions and have something attached to her.

I knew and understood the precautions Meka wanted to take; just hearing she was pregnant had me ready to tell the world. I put my hand over my face in shame.

"What's wrong?" Meka asked.

"I regret that I cheated on you, and I'm sorry for putting all the extra stress on you, too." Meka tried to stop me, but I needed to get it out.

"I am sorry TaMeka. I should have been down with you and worried about only you, but I had to go out and do other stuff... stupid stuff," I confessed. "I understand if you don't want to be with me, but I will be in my child's life."

Meka cried happy tears, "Okay. Thank you."

Chapter 14
Krystal

*O*MG, *I cannot believe this. I am pregnant, and I have yet to determine who the father is.*

I knew I was careless, but why did I have to be *this* careless? *Shoot.*

"Is everything okay?" I heard from the other side of the door."

I opened it to let Meka in and showed her the pregnancy test. I knew she would be the last one to judge. She looked at it, and tears started to form in her eyes. I knew it was because she couldn't have kids, but she was happy for me.

Meka came over and hugged me. "It will be okay."

I hugged my cousin back. "Thank you. That explains my cravings for chicken wings with hot sauce."

Meka laughed. I told her first, I thought it was my period, but now I knew why.

"Are you going to tell David?"

I hunched my shoulders. David deserved to know, but he also needed to know it could be another man's child, and I did not want to get his hopes up for nothing.

"I guess it's fair that he at least knows what's going on," I answered, then got an idea. "I will tell him at his job."

"That's a great idea!" Meka exclaimed.

"It's safer. David will react differently there."

I knew I could have told him at home, but I would have to stab, shoot, or do something to him afterward. David knew how to act around people, so I took my chances at his office.

I took the day off to take care of business. I showered and got ready to start my day, running errands I'd put off for weeks. Deciding to wear a dress, I chose one that fell just below my knees with a pair of black flats and accessorized it with a jewelry set Angela gave me after pulling my hair into a ponytail. It was hot outside, and I knew the humidity was going to kick up.

"Who is this girl walking down the hall?" Meka asked.

I sprang around and started twerking. Meka began to do the same thing, and we burst into laughter. I looked at myself in the oversized mirror located in my living room and grabbed my purse.

"Wish me luck."

"Krystal, wait," said Meka. "I want to tell you that I am pregnant, too."

I jumped for joy. "Are you for real, Meka? Like for real, pregnant?"

Meka laughed. "Yes. Yes, for real."

I hugged her.

"Krystal, don't get too excited. I do not want to get my hopes up. Don't tell anyone, either."

Meka and I hugged again. "I understand, and I know you are happy on the inside. We are going to pray and keep our hopes up. Okay?"

I took Meka by the hand and said a prayer.

"Thank you, Krystal?"

"You're welcome, Meka. Does Carl know about this?"

Meka looked at me. "Yes. We have actually been talking more."

That was all news to me. "Is it a good thing?" I asked.

Meka's eyes wandered. "I don't know. This is his child, and he knows he messed up. It's just that he abandoned the trust I had for him. Krystal, he abandoned everything that I had for him—everything. I just don't know."

"To be honest, I don't think Carl will start back over from scratch."

I thought about my words. No matter how much someone loves someone else, their loyalty will determine their true destiny.

"Go ahead, Krystal," Meka interrupted my thoughts. "Get your fast self out of here. I am going to meet up with Carl."

Meka gave me a thumb's up. "If you need me, call me."

I hugged her one last time and told Meka congratulations; I was happy for them. I prayed it would all work out for the best. Afterward, I left and got in my car. I decided to send Malcolm a text letting him know we needed to talk and drove to David's job.

I prayed I was not carrying David's child. I wasn't sure how Malcolm would react, but I did not want to ruin anything going on with us. In six months, he had become my soulmate. For the child to be David's, the relationship between Malcolm and me would be destroyed.

I also prayed that David would not act a fool. I needed him to be cool about all of this. I pulled up to his office building and parked in the visitor's parking, then walked in. Some of David's colleagues greeted me, and I gave them all a dry wave. That did not stop Sarah from coming over, trying to talk to me.

Sarah was always the type who wanted to be in your business. It was not a surprise when she stopped to try and see what was going on with David and me. I chit-chatted with her before going farther to meet David. When I arrived on the 6th floor, I was relieved that his assistant wasn't there.

"May I help you?" a young lady asked from behind the desk. I read her name tag, and it showed Mya. I knew she was new.

I extended my hand out and introduced myself as David's fiancée.

"Oh, sorry, Ms. Jackson. Would you like me to give him a call?"

Krystal quickly responded, "No, and just call me Krystal. I would like to go back to his office and surprise him."

Not waiting for an answer from Mya, I walked in the direction of David's office. When I got there, the door was cracked. I tried to listen to hear if David was on a business call handling something before I went in. One thing about him was that he could play the professionalism card well.

The sound of moaning distracted me. Whoever it was, they were giving David the business. I opened the door wider and walked in. David had his assistant, Lela, bent the fuck over. He was fucking her like he did not have a wife at home. I, for one, surely wasn't going to tell her about Bertha and those damn kids."

I stood and watched for half a second, then David and I made eye contact. He immediately stopped, and then Lela and I made eye contact. They both scurried around to get their clothes to put back on. I laughed.

"Don't do that," I interrupted. "I'm just here to tell you I am pregnant, and this could *possibly* be your baby."

David squinted, "What do you mean, possibly?"

"Well, do you see what you have going on here?" I questioned, pointing to David and his assistant. "Well, I had my own situation. The only thing is, I was smart about mine and kept it under wrap. I knew y'all were screwing all along."

He scrunched up his face, and so did Lela. I turned, then looked at her. "Next time you want to fuck, do not leave the door cracked, and make sure not to get caught red-handed."

With that, I walked out and left the door just like it was. I didn't let my emotions get in the way of anything. David did not care about anyone but himself. I had left him already, so I prayed and hoped I did not have to see or deal with him anymore.

I walked out to the parking lot, and my phone started ringing. I answered Malcolm's FaceTime. *This man gets sexier every time I see him.* Malcolm was at work, so I couldn't brag on what he had on. It could've been just a brown shirt and an apron, and he still would've looked good.

Over the months of knowing him, I had learned plenty about Malcolm and how he really made his money. Many people would have suspected he was a drug dealer, but I knew he was smart and secretive about what he does. Malcolm is a businessman, and he handled his business well. *I hope Malcolm really takes this news in a good way.*

"What? You just gonna stare at the screen, Krystal? You are rude, girl." Malcolm smiled, showing his white teeth.

No longer distracted, I laughed. "Malcolm, I am pregnant," I blurted out.

The biggest smiled crossed his face. That was the hardest I'd ever seen him smile, but it was short-lived.

"Is it mine?"

His smile broke, and I shrugged my shoulders. "I don't know, Malcolm."

"Do you want it to be mine?"

I briefly avoided the question. I do, but it is a huge possibility that David could still be in the picture.

"I haven't been with David since that night at my parents' house. Honestly, I don't know when the last time we fucked was," I finally answered.

"Well, that shit bet not have been recent."

Now, it was my turn to frown. I turned up my nose in return.

"Malcom, you know what it is between you and I. Why would I step out on you?"

He looked at me on the screen.

"You know it's not recent, Malcolm. David does know, so it is only a matter of time before we can tell."

I saw David and Lela walking out with boxes. "Malcolm, talk to me."

"It's nothing, baby girl," he responded. "I can't trip because I knew what I was getting myself in. I pray this is my baby. I will take care of you and my child. Ya' heard me?"

I smiled at him because I knew he was telling the truth. Whenever we would go out to a restaurant, shopping, or even a movie, I did not have to pay for a thing. I couldn't remember the last time I even paid rent. Malcolm took care of that.

"Well, just to let you know, I am about to max out your black card."

Malcolm laughed because he knew it was the truth. "Well, when your shit starts getting declined, then you will know what it is."

Malcolm's name was getting called, so I knew he had to go back to work. We said our good-byes, and I started my car. Leaving the visitor's parking lot at David's job, I decided to get something from a local chicken shack. I was serious about my craving, although I wasn't sure if that's what they were. I just wanted chicken; then, I planned to sit home and lounge for the rest of the day.

Chapter 15
Meka

I cannot believe this. I am pregnant. To be honest, I have faith in this pregnancy and only thought I couldn't have kids because of an abortion at 15 years old. After that, the doctors told me I couldn't conceive.

On a cold night in my foster home, my mother, Mrs. Ryan, must have gotten mad at Mr. Ryan and turned off the heat. The bad part about it was I was the one who had to suffer. Sometimes, I could have sworn they didn't know I was in the house.

I was placed in different foster homes since I was two years old. People would say I was a bad child because I stole, but the worst part was getting told I was too dark. I considered myself light-skinned, not extremely dark, or even dark at all. However, compared to the Ryan's, I was too dark for their family.

When I got placed at the Ryan resident, everything went smoothly. I would have thought this was somewhere I could lay my head and not be worried, but one night during one of Mr. and Mrs. Ryan's arguments, I went downstairs to sneak some snacks and bottled water. Mrs. Ryan could be petty, and she would throw out or lock the snack foods with everything else in cabinets. Sometimes, she would cook what she liked, knowing damn well nobody else ate her dry ass spaghetti.

I had just gotten out of the shower and was wearing shorts that stopped below my knees. For a 15-year-old, I had a lot of booty. Mr. Ryan walked through the kitchen on his way to the basement and immediately stopped. I did not hear footsteps or him going down the stairs, so I was curious. I turned around and saw him staring at me with lust in his eyes.

Instantly, I felt uncomfortable and grabbed my stuff, trying to move around the dining room table. Since I was a chubby girl, that was nearly impossible; however, I did it the best way I could, and before going upstairs, Mr. Ryan grabbed my arm.

"I want you for dessert," he told me.

I immediately ran up the stairs. I could hear Mrs. Ryan yell, "Stop running up my stairs."

Every night for two months, I slept with knives and any other sharp object I could find that would be a weapon. Still, Mr. Ryan peeped what I was doing and left me alone until, one night, I came home from volleyball practice sweating and stinking. I put my stuff down and got my sleeping clothes. When I turned on the water and got in the shower, five minutes later, Mr. Ryan pulled the curtain back and put his hand over my mouth.

"Oh, you thought I was not going to get any pussy."

I started shivering because I did not know what he was capable of. I prayed he would take his hand off my mouth, but that prayer went unanswered. Then I noticed the heater was on, and no one would hear me anyway if I screamed. That heater was loud, and I knew Mrs. Ryan, or no one else would believe me otherwise.

Mr. Ryan stuck his dick right in my hole, and I immediately screamed out and cried. I was a virgin, so imagine having a dick slammed in you with no remorse, feelings, or anything. I took it and took it for what seemed like hours. He eventually pulled out, and my vagina was just there. I felt disgusted and humiliated. I sat in the shower for 15 minutes, crying and hating myself. I wondered why my mom gave me up to live this lifestyle. I just knew she was out doing whatever she wanted to do.

I got up and cleaned myself off. Then I got out of the shower to get dressed and grabbed the knife I always had hidden in my dresser draw. The knife didn't do anything because it was a repeated cycle. Mrs. Ryan acted clueless to everything.

...TWO MONTHS LATER

"Why are you in here throwing the fuck up?"
Mrs. Ryan asked me for a third time this
morning.

The only thing I could do was shrug my
shoulders. "Lately, I have been feeling
nauseous.

"You bet not be out here trying to act fast.
You will go back to the group home, messing
around with me."

I rolled my eyes. Ever since that night, she
said I had a change in my behavior. Well, if it
weren't for the fact that her husband was
fucking me every time he got a chance, I would
not have been going through that.

After that night, I lost count of how many
times we fucked. I mean literally, it was more of
him touching me, and I just accepted it. It
happened day after day and week after week.
Whenever Mrs. Ryan would leave and not let me
go, it would happen. I sat there and overheard

her say something about pregnancy, but I did not believe her.

"Here, take this." Mrs. Ryan handed me a pregnancy stick and a cup. "You pee in this plastic cup; then you stick the pregnancy test inside the cup and follow the directions."

She walked out of the bathroom. I was in there for 10 minutes at most, scared shitless. I remember being just afraid to look at the results. I already knew but wondered what would happen after that. About three minutes later, it read pregnancy.

"Meka," I heard Mrs. Ryan yell.

"Come in."

I knew I was going back to the group home. She looked at me in disbelief.

"So, who's baby is this?"

I paused because I did not want to say the wrong thing. I shrugged my shoulders.

"I am not going to ask you anymore."

That's when I knew the truth would come out. I pointed to Mr. Ryan, her husband, and she busted out laughing.

"Girl, if anything, you wanted him." It was my turn to look at her in disgust. "Come on; your social worker is on her way to get you."

I started packing my stuff, and I stood by the door. Ten minutes later, Mrs. Carly pulled up, and I met her outside. Of course, she asked me a thousand and one questions. She talked to Mrs. and Mr. Ryan, and then we went to the group home.

"Are you going to keep the baby or abort it?"

I never responded, but as you can see, I do not have any children.

Chapter 16
David

"Hold up. That can *possibly* be another man's baby?" Lela asked me in disgust.

I nodded my head, "Yes."

Krystal gave me a taste of my own medicine. To be honest, I didn't want to be around Bertha anymore. She had let herself go and was looking more disgusting by the second. As for the kids, I am still in their lives; I'm not going to let my babies go.

The night I was in the house with Krystal and her man, I heard them fucking. I wanted to cock-block but didn't feel like fighting. The next morning they disappeared; now Krystal says she's pregnant. I know it isn't my child; we haven't fucked in ages.

Lela moving around brought me out of my thoughts. "Are you still paying for Jamaya's classes?" she asked.

"Yes."

Now that the truth was out, I can come out too. I had a child with Lela. My marriage that would have been with Krystal would have been a cover-up for her parents.

The one thing I forgot was that it would hurt my three children. They would always ask, "Daddy, when are you coming home?" That bothered me, so I knew I had to put a stop to it, but how?

I never expected Krystal to come that day, but she never shed a tear before she left. It was more of a whatever type of thing. If it were my child, I would be a parent, but I have been with Krystal for damn near four years and counting, and we never made kids. To be honest, I thought I could not have a child before Bertha got pregnant; that, or something was wrong with Krystal's uterus. Lela was now pregnant with her second child, my fifth, and now I begged to differ. It definitely wasn't me.

Lela came up to me and kissed me on the lips. I am not going to lie; I love big girls, and Lela was my type. She was chubby with long hair that I loved grabbing while hitting it from the back. I kissed Lela back. Now I can go home and finally be with my family.

"Dad," all my children yelled. It had been a while since I'd been there, and things had changed. My youngest daughter was reaching her hands out, so I could pick her up. That is what life is all about. I told Bertha to take them to my mom's house. Mom brought them over to my house.

"I am going to get dinner started," Lela whispered to me. I nodded and went to spend time with my children.

"Now, you have to make up your mind, son."

Chapter 17
Malcolm

“Boss, I need you to help me with the line.”

“Okay,” I said.

I finished talking to my baby girl for a minute and told her I had to go. Here I was filling in for my cousin, Rico, today. You might as well call me the fill-in man, but this is something I did on a regular. *Family helps family.* But on the real, let's rewind to that conversation.

“A baby. Am I somebody's father?” I asked myself.

I am happy and appalled at the same time. I knew there was a possibility it could be David's, but I think I overruled all those chances. Even after the first encounter, I was freely nutting in her. Krystal asked about a condom, but let's just say it never happened.

I am not going to lie; I am feeling Krystal. The way she carries herself and doesn't indulge in drama, I love that about a female. I don't need to hear about that all the time.

Honestly, the way I have gotten to know Krystal is deeper than her ex has ever gone. She loves to read, and she is a super freak. Laughing at that part, she also likes to take long walks on the beach, and her favorite place is Red Lobsters, the only thing it seems we've eaten since we had been intimate. I know she loves flowers, and she enjoys being creative. I just love the girl.

My mom tried to get in contact with me, but I'm not talking to her at this moment. The one thing I hate is a liar, and that she was. I got in touch with the prison that my "supposed to be" dad is in, and he agreed to see me. Tomorrow, I'm going to meet him for the 5th time in my life. I met this man, and I cannot even process why I got lied to like this. Now that I think about it, he disappeared after he and my mom got into an argument. I don't know about what, but he never came back around.

...THE NEXT DAY

I drove five hours to meet the man who could possibly be my father. He was in a prison in Memphis; I couldn't tell you the name if I wanted to. I sat at a table for about 30 minutes battling with my feelings. I was never a feelings type of person, but man, this situation could take a whole other turn in a matter of seconds.

James walked to the table I was sitting at and took a seat. He looked at me, and this man looked like he wanted to cry, but he held his composure.

"Hello, Malcolm," he spoke with a deep voice that matched mine.

I nodded my head and wanted to get to the real reason I was there. "Are you my biological father?"

"Yes," he said, "and I will explain." James put his head down.

"Your mom and I were messing around. Everything was going well," he started. "There weren't any feelings attached or no sexually transmitted diseases coming our way. Avery, the guy she was seeing, was doing time in prison for murder, and one day we decided to take it to the next level.

She said she told Avery she was through with him, and when he got out, he could only be there for the children. That was a lie. Avery ended up getting released earlier than what I expected, and I walked in to see your mom fucking the man. Like, dead fucking him—like she didn't just fuck me two hours before.

That hurt my heart, but I was a man about it. I came back to get my stuff for her to tell me she was pregnant and didn't know who the father was."

I listened intently and thought about Krystal. She didn't know who the father was, but I was there. David wasn't just going to show up and jump back in to claim nothing.

Malcolm continued, "I walked away, but that did not stop me from going to doctor's appointments and being there when your mother had you. Can you imagine two niggas in one room trying to see what you look like?" *I had no idea but would soon find out.*

"You had stopped breathing 26 seconds afterward," he told me. "Once they got your breathing back by doing CPR, you were rushed to the intensive care unit and monitored for six days until you could breathe on your own. I came and saw you every day. Let's just say I knew you were mine. I was going to go back and sign the birth certificate, but I end up getting locked up for something that happened two years prior. I pleaded and pleaded with your mother to let me sign it, but that didn't work.

The whole time Avery was taking credit for my work.

I came by and saw you while I was out on bail. Your mom and I had a huge argument about me being in your life. She kept calling me a criminal and said I was a fugitive, but I knew that was Avery getting in her head. Your mom can be naive at times, and she was very vulnerable in this situation. I knew once I kissed your forehead and left the house, that would be the last time I would see you.

When they moved me here, I pleaded with her to send me pictures of your growth. Don't let your mom fool you; she got money whenever she needed it. She just chooses to cut me off and do things her way."

I looked at him and could not do anything but shake my head. I was wondering why my mother was always affectionate with me.

"Do I have any other brothers and sisters?" I asked.

James shook his head yes and gave me the name Carl Woodland. I shook my head again.

"Look, I know you don't know me, Malcolm, but I am willing to get to know you. I have six years left, and I would like for you to meet Carl. I understand that this is a lot, so I just want you to take your time and think about this."

I nodded and chatted it up the last 30 minutes I had left with James. I told him about a possible baby with this girl I'm really feeling. I'm not going to lie and say I was feeling better than I was before I went out there, but I had answers now.

I FaceTimed my mom in the parking lot, and she answered on the first ring. To my surprise, Avery was with her. I was not going to bust her bubble because I could care less at this point.

"Mom, I talked to my birth father."

Her eyes were big as a nut, but I was not going to say much more.

"Well, son, did you get answers?"

"Yes."

Even though my mom lied to me, I still respected her as my mother. I was just disappointed that she could not come and talk to me. I spoke to that man as if I knew him for years. I knew I was protected. If he was making stuff happen while he was in jail, that let me know a lot about her.

"I was just calling to tell you that I met him, and we are cool."

My mom was ecstatic and surprised at the same damn time. I cannot lie and say I didn't love her. Sometimes our actions can just get in front of things. I chopped it up with her, and then headed home.

Chapter 18
Krystal

"Ooh, get this baby the hell out of me," I screamed.

Hell, I was ready to deliver, and I only dilated at a 5. Meka was at my bedside looking scared as hell. I don't know why when her ass was about to go through the same shit in less than two fucking months.

I felt another contraction hit, and I mentally told myself I would not have any more kids. If Malcolm had something to do with it, there would be another one coming soon.

"Krystal, in all honesty, didn't no one tell you to be fucking."

"Fuck you, Malcolm."

That was his idea for me to go natural. Well, my idea too, but it felt better to blame him for now. *It was good for the body, etc. Bullshit, I will not do this again.*

Malcolm came over to me and rubbed my back. It was smoothing for the time being. The nurse, Mrs. Angel, came in to assist me. I was too far along for the epidural, which I did not care about because I was going natural. She took my vitals and asked to check my cervix. I was relieved she told me I was another centimeter dilated. That means I had four more to go, and I was pushing.

I decided to text David and let him know I was in labor. He deserved to know because this could be his child. When I first found out I was pregnant, I got on my knees, and I prayed to God that this was Malcolm's child. I did not want anything to do with David. Ever since I caught him and his assistant, I kept him updated on the baby. Once I find out who the father is, I can go from there.

Malcolm put my hand over my head and gave me a cold towel because I was burning up. Meka went to fill my ice cup up for the 50th time. Carl sat back and prayed the baby didn't come any time soon.

"Meka, we gonna cancel your labor. I can't go through this with you."

We all laughed. Carl looked scared as hell, and he had three kids.

I never really liked ice until I got pregnant. Throughout my whole pregnancy, I craved ice chips, chicken, and Red Lobster. I knew Malcolm was getting tired of eating at those places, but I could try something else and regretted it when I get home.

I got up and decided to walk around to dilate more. Malcolm and Meka were right by my side. I felt another sharp pain, so I immediately held on to Meka, while I laid back down.

Dr. Crowhne walked in and assisted me with my cervix. He told me I was ready to have a baby. I was relieved and scared at the same damn time. They prepped me, and the nurse insisted everything would be okay.

"Okay, when I count to three, I need a big push," the doctor said. "1,2,3... Push."

I pushed and screamed. Then I stopped. They started counting to 10, and then they stopped. The nurse did it again. I did that about 20 times, then there was a cry. I was relieved. That took a lot out of me on so many levels.

I took a deep breath and laid my head back. Malcolm grabbed me another cold towel and wiped my face, then put one on top of my head. It's was a girl. Malcolm cut the umbilical cord, and they brought him up to me, holding her so I could see. I took one look at her, and I already knew who's baby it was. I just needed a DNA test to prove it.

We were all amazed at the same time. I just pushed out a 7lb 8oz baby, 11 inches long. The nurse took my baby girl to clean her up while I delivered the afterbirth and got stitched up.

"Malia is her name," I told Malcolm.

Malcolm held her in his arms. She already had him wrapped around her fingers, and he knew he was in trouble.

...A DAY LATER.

This room was awkward as ever. I could not make this up if I wanted to. I had my parents, David, his parents, David's assistant, Malcolm, Meka, and Carl, in one room. We were waiting for the test results, and I just wanted to go home. Honestly, I didn't know why my parents were there. My guess was they just wanted to be nosey and have something to talk about. Everyone saw Malia, and of course, people had their own opinions, but I could care less.

While we waited for the results, I reflected. To update you guys on everything, I had not talked to my parents since they were talking to my neighbor. They had not checked on me, and I knew the only way they knew I was pregnant was because David had told them. What bothered me was they were more in tune with Lela than anything. They were talking to her like she was replacing me, but I did not care enough to keep worrying about it.

David told me how he was married to her now, and they had kids. I am not going to lie and say it didn't hurt, but I got over it when I had sex with Malcolm. How he already had a wife, a fiancée, and a whole girlfriend made no sense.

Meka and Carl were working on their relationship, and I was happy for her. I honestly thought she was going to leave him and start over, but I guess she knew where her heart was.

Malcolm and I are as solid as they come. I found confidence and a love for new things, including loving myself better. I don't work at the bank anymore, either. I work for Malcolm as an accountant. *Can you talk about relationship goals?*

There was a knock at the door. Nurse Angel came in, and she felt the tension. I could tell she was nervous, but we all were. She had two envelopes and opened one of them.

"David Jackson?" David raised his hand, and that got my full attention. "You are not the father."

I could tell David was pissed, but again I did not care. I did not have to deal with his sorry ass no more. *Good, fucking, bye.*

They never left; I knew they wanted to be nosey.

"Malcolm Woodland, you are the father."

Malcolm hugged me. "Thank you for giving me my first daughter," he gushed.

I was ecstatic, and I knew we could do this parenting thing together.

Chapter 19
Carl

I was ecstatic for Malcolm and Krystal. I don't know how she stuck with David for so long anyways. If you looked at the two of them, you would not think love was there; they were the total opposite. When I heard that last name, Meka looked at me, and I finally found my brother.

When Malcolm made that visit down to see my dad, I got a call. Dad told me everything. I cannot hold a grudge for what his mom did or how he found out, but I am here now, and that's all that matters.

"Meka, I will be right back."

Meka nodded her head, and I told Malcolm to come here. The first thing I had to do was tell him congratulations because that was his daughter by his looks, touch, and everything.

After that, I had started the conversation off about how my pops had contacted me and told me he was my brother. I had sat on the information because I didn't know how to tell him.

Malcolm nodded his head. I took one look at him, and he looked just like our father. We hugged each other, and I had a feeling that this was going to make us tighter than anything. When I was growing up, my pops always told me I had another sibling. When he got locked up, I was 15 years old, and that's when he had decided to come clean and tell me everything. He said, "I don't know where he is, but trust me, one day y'all will meet." I didn't know what to say, but I was looking, and that's how I honestly found Meka. I could stop looking now. If it was meant to be, then it was meant to be.

"Move David. Nobody has time for you," we heard coming from Krystal's hospital room

Malcolm ran into the room, and I followed suit. Meka was trying to keep David from getting to Krystal. *Please do not ask me what happened within 10 minutes.*

We heard David screaming and calling Krystal out of her name. Malcolm got in David's face and said, "Do it again."

That is the first time in my life I had ever seen David fold under another man. That shit was funny, and I started laughing. Krystal and Meka did the same thing. Of course, the whole family got up and left, which left four of us in the room.

I had to tell the girls about Malcolm and me being related. They were excited. Meka started talking about double dates and all of this other stuff. I mean, these girls were speaking a whole new language.

"Knock Knock."

A nurse walked in with baby Malia Woodland. I don't know how to say her name, but I am going to give her a name. Malia is not hard, but I want to be different.

Chapter 20
Malcolm

To say a nigga was ecstatic was an understatement. I had my first daughter, and Malia found my brother. To be honest, I think that was my only brother. I never asked because I was not a big fan of meeting people.

My father and I's relationship got closer. I let him video chat and see his granddaughter, and this nigga went into tears. I bet when he went to the back, he straightened up.

As for my mom, I talk to her every once in a while. She decided that if I speak to my father, she did not want to be bothered with me. I told her everything my father said to me about her, and she was mad. She just kept saying he is lying, etc.

She and Avery are still together, and they were due to get married any day. Uncle Ray accepted it and was cool because he still had access to whatever crazy kind of relationship the three of them were in. I was told by one of my siblings that they were having a courthouse wedding where Uncle Ray was the best man, being that he's Avery's best friend, and a reception afterward, and I can come. Sadly, my mom cut that off and said she did not want me there. With that, I stayed my black ass at home watching TV. I saw pictures on Facebook, but that was about it.

My daughter is going on a month now, and she was just as beautiful as they come. I noticed she took after me with her curly hair, but she had her momma's eyes. I knew that would be a problem, but those eyes could have a new car if she asked. I just was *not* going to tell her that.

I walked into the bedroom and sanitized my hands, then I went to Malia Nicole Woodland and put a sheet over my clothes, then I laid her on top of me while I fixed her a bottle. Once she started eating, I relaxed and enjoyed the silence.

"You know you will have some boys after you, and your mom will not hesitate to shoot them."

She stopped drinking her bottle and looked up at me. The smile I had been waiting for appeared; she made my night.

Malia went back to finish drinking. I looked up and saw Krystal recording. *It is amazing how she just pops up out of anywhere.* I bet if I went through her phone, she would have all the memories, and not tell me.

Krystal sat on the love seat and put her head on my shoulder.

"I love you, Malcolm."

"I love you too, Krystal."

Chapter 21
David

"You guys are having a girl," Jackie, the nurse informed us. I was thrilled, but if this keeps happening, I was out-numbered.

I bet y'all were wondering what happened when I left the hospital. Well, my wife and I went home and cleaned out the whole house that Krystal and I shared. We put everything up for sale, and surprisingly it sold within two months.

I followed them on Facebook, and I can honestly admit that Krystal looks happy. The baby did not do any harm in any of this. I had a whole plan in my head on what I was going to do if this child was not mine, but seeing the way Malcolm was over Krystal made me just abort the mission and keep going. *My* wife, Lela, and I drove separate cars since we both had to work. I kissed her, and I was on my merry way.

Bertha and I got a divorce. I was only there for the children, but she didn't complain. She decided it was time to let me go. Things were okay at home, but we were still rocky, and sometimes I questioned my love for her, but I will try my all with this one.

My family and Krystal's family adore Lela; they like her to the fullest. When I told them the truth, both sides were happy for me. Krystal's parents never mention her, and I think they stopped talking to her. Everything is good over here.

Chapter 22
Meka

To say I was excited was an understatement. My cousin, Krystal, finally had her baby, and I can admit I was scared. Since I found out I was pregnant, I have settled down with Carl. We were still rocky, but it was better than before. I was having a healthy pregnancy, and that is all I could ask for.

I looked at my ringing cellphone to see Carl's baby momma calling me. I ignored it for her to call right back. Ever since Carl picked up Carl, Jr., he has not gone back. Carl found out some of the stuff Riya was doing, and he did want his son around that, so he gained full custody. That left her looking stupid because that money stopped, and I knew she was after the money when she got pregnant by him in the first place.

Of course, she was upset, but who cares. I now have a three-year-old son, and I am waiting for them to prep me for my C-section. My doctor did not want me to deliver naturally. He was afraid I would lose a lot of blood and might not make it out. When Carl heard that, he immediately decided for me. I could not be mad because my life could possibly be in danger.

"How are you doing, girl?" Carl asked me for the 5th time.

I knew he was nervous, and I was trying to calm him down and keep me calm too. Jaheim, Jr. was staying with Krystal and Malcolm. Once it was safe, they would bring him to the hospital. It was funny because we literally went from no kids, a broken homes, and hiding secrets to having kids and being a family now.

Nurse Maria came in to assist me, and then she and Carl took me up to get this baby out of me. I was proud of my baby. We made it this long, and I prayed everything was successful. Two hours later, I had a beautiful baby girl.

Oh, my gosh, she is adorable at 8lbs 6 oz. and 13 inches. I knew she got the height from her dad. I was so in love with her. Since Carl was in the room, you know he had to do a photoshoot. Wait until the pictures come, he is about to be creative. Genesis Marie Woodland is her name.

Krystal, Jaheim, Jr., Malcolm, and Malia came running into the room. Genesis immediately started crying, and Jaheim, Jr. felt bad. He put hand sanitizer on his hands and quickly went over to his baby sister. Since he didn't know how to say her name, he called her Gen. It was funny and cute.

About the Author

A native of Chicago, Illinois, Zina is a graduate of Mid State College in Peoria, Illinois, where she studied Applied Science and is now a medical assistant. Her pastimes include writing, for which she has always had a passion.

At the age of 12, Zina started writing and penned her first novel when she was 15 years old. While she had big dreams, she doubted herself equally, so nothing came of it. However, one day she set a goal to finish writing and to become a published author. That day is here now. May this, her first novel, inspire you to join her in continuing to strive to let nothing get in the way.

Made in the USA
Columbia, SC
06 November 2020